MY BLUE
SKIN LOVER

MONONA WALI

ISBN 978-0-9831191-7-3

Grateful acknowledgement is made to Penguin Books for permission
to reprint select poems of Akka Mahadevi from *Speaking of Śiva*,
translated by A. K. Ramanujan, copyright © 1973 by A. K. Ramanujan.
Reproduced by permission of Penguin Books, Ltd.

Published in the United States by
Blue Jay Ink, 451 A East Ojai Ave., Ojai, California 93023
bluejayink.com

for the blue,
unbidden

SHIVA

is the Hindu god of life and death, of destruction and rebirth.
He is terrifying, and he is benevolent.

Shiva has three eyes through which he can view the past,
the present, and the future.

The third eye looks inward. If he were to open it,
the searing heat would scorch all of creation.

"And when he possessed her they seemed to swoon together at the very borderland of life's mystery."

—Kate Chopin

1

I need cumin seeds. And turmeric. And ground coriander. Indo-Pak is restocking shelves, and half-emptied boxes are jamming up the aisles. Why, I wonder, can't they do this early in the morning and not when people are trying to rush home and get dinner on the table? The summer heat has intensified the scents. There's just one little fan whirring like a jet propeller, and that's where the shopkeeper is sitting, chewing on her betel nut, watching a Hindi movie on a small color television. A garbled female voice sings. I translate in my head. *Your heart has lodged in mine like grooves in a stone. Difficult to escape from this; how would I escape if I wished to?* I hum along. Escape. Escape. Lush poetry. It chases me wherever I go. So does love, the nature of love, love as it relates to a bunch of long-dead, mystic Indian saints who are the subject of my Ph.D., which I can't seem to finish, or escape. What was the line I translated just before I left my office? *He paralyzed my will, ravished my body, took my pleasure as payment, took over all of me.*

Get home. Cook dinner. What would please Zoo tonight? Will he want to ravish my flesh? Will I want him to? Something light, cool, refreshing. Nothing fried, no heavy sauces. Actually I don't want to cook at all. Nothing appeals. All my enthusiasms have dried up. Rebecca Leigh's attempted suicide weighs on me. She was my closest ally and friend in the department. When I visited her in the hospital two days ago, it was all I could do to walk out. Her ashen face was turned to the wall and excavated of life. And Safiyah quit altogether six months ago, just months from finishing his thesis on the genesis of the Koran. He is living with his parents in Long Island and working in the local supermarket until substitute teaching opens up in the public school. Both had Vanderoe as their advisor. Yesterday Vanderoe told me I was his last Ph.D. candidate. I couldn't tell from the look in his eye if he was challenging me to quit or continue. To say you've seen evil in someone's eyes seems overblown, but it's as close as I've come.

I unload my weighed-down shoulder bag on one of the boxes so I can reach up for the flattened rice. It will make a good, quick summer dish if I mix it with non-fat yogurt. This morning Zoo woke up in a good mood and reached over in bed and nibbled on my shoulder. Made a strange little eek, eek, eek crying noise and told me that's how an osprey calls its love mate. I shoved him away. Ignored the momentary hurt that rippled through him. How can you make jokes when others are falling all around you? Ah, dear husband. I adorned him with the nickname Zoo. He charmed me with animal calls. It is what he learned as a ten-year-old, outcast as a fat boy, alone in his room with a tape of animal calls. Mimicry. He's so good at it. Now he's a lean and furiously ambitious stockbroker. Loves Slim-Fast.

I fill up my plastic basket and take it to the counter. I've gotten too much. At least the pantry will be full even as I become witness to my own slow emptying.

"No rotis," I sort of ask the owner, but mostly tell her. My mother still makes the whole-wheat flatbread from scratch almost every day.

"No rotis," she shakes her head. "Too, too hot," she says, although I don't think the heat has anything to do with it. The rotis are made in some factory in Queens. Everything on her is droopy, as if she wilted long ago in the heat. Her cheeks, her eyes, and her neck flesh sag; her shoulders drop off precipitously. "No good weather. Ankles swelling. Look. See." And she comes around from behind the counter and lifts the pant legs of her frayed *salwar* and shows me a swollen, plump foot with a puffy ankle that looks like a filled-up water balloon.

"Sit down with your legs up," I advise her.

"When sit? No time. Son no good. No help."

"I know. I know." We are not exactly friends, but I've been in here enough times that she can share news of her ailments, which seem inexhaustible, and the disappointments of her son.

She loads my purchases in a plastic bag. There's a tray of samosas set out on the counter, perfect pyramids stuffed with spicy potato and pea filling and fried to a golden crispiness. She sees me looking at them and asks, "You want?"

"No," I tell her, "not this time." I've had them before, and they are tasty and not too greasy, but if I bring them home Zoo will protest. He doesn't want the temptation.   I pull my wallet from my purse and pay up, and head out onto 96th Street as another song follows me. *We were destined to meet, beloved; love was destined to bloom. In my eyes, in my breath, there is you and only you, beloved.*

2

The woman goes down like a building. She's big, buxom, and moaning.

"Oh, ooh, oh, girl," she says, looking at me, desperate. I'm not half a block from Indo-Pak. My arm flies out, but she is more than I can handle. Down she topples, onto her pile of cardboard, on top of the watches, scarves, handbags, windup robots, and whatever else she is selling that day. I go down with her; slow motion, my shoulder bag and purchases colliding with the sidewalk. She clutches her chest. I right myself and kneel down next to her. She grips my hand.

"Is it your heart?"

"Oh, oh, oh," she says, with pain. She's gasping, short of breath.

A blond man wheeling a carry-on suitcase stops, flips the lid of his cell phone, dials 911. "A woman is having a heart attack on the street." He barks the coordinates. "Ninety-sixth and Amsterdam." He has a military-style crew cut and has the stocky build of a bulldog, all muscles and sinew. He could easily handle her, but he keeps his distance. Others walk by, hesitate, move on. Do they think I have the situation covered?

I know this woman. I have walked by her many times. I nicknamed her Jangles long ago because her arms are always covered with bracelets—thick silver ornaments—that run the length of her arm from wrist to bicep. She conducts business on Amsterdam Avenue not far from our apartment. She sits on a lawn chair with odd bits of merchandise spread about her, hammers and hairnets and maps of Yugoslavia and the USSR and other places that don't exist anymore. I once bought a used Burmese–English dictionary from her. She is like discarded newspaper. Sprays of gray and black frizzy hair that looks like sheep fuzz spill forth between the cracks of her ill-wrapped turban. She has a boxy transistor radio, and out of it I hear the squawk of some minister preaching.

She grabs my arm. Even if her heart muscle is giving out, her hand isn't. She has me like a vice, and she isn't going to let go. She looks at me, and I see her eyes are cloudy with pain. Then she becomes still—her eyes open and shut in slow motion. I look around, panicked. Oh, please don't die, I think. "Please, please, please," I whisper. I invoke Shiva, god of life and death, god of my dead saints, to come to her aid. I pray to him. I have never prayed before. I feel an expansive love for Jangles as I stare into her pained face, this person I do not know except as a creature of the street. I want her to live.

The blond man stands about five paces away, looking up and down the street. His self-appointed task is to watch for the ambulance, but clearly he isn't going to get his hands dirtied. A crowd starts to form. *Hey, someone is down over here.* Shopkeepers step from their stores, and someone comes close, a man with a blue baseball cap and a royal-blue T-shirt.

"Let us get to work," he says to me. I startle at his voice. It's thick and low and musical.

He tears open the clothes around her chest. First a vest, then a shirt, then I help him with some kind of undershirt that we have to pull up, then a bra. It's August, and normal people are going sleeveless. Finally we come to the brown of her chest. Smooth chocolate-pudding skin, a few shades darker than my own. Her big breasts are slung lazily to each side like nothing is happening, and her smell is thick and pungent. Exotic oils, musk maybe, or sandalwood. Or is it the man who has come to the rescue? He gives off a wonderful floral smell.

"Mouth to mouth," he whispers, as if we were in a library. He takes my hand and pinches her nose with it. His hand is warm, and its gentleness makes me feel courageous. I look at him, and I have to look away quickly. His eyes sear me.

"Breathe!" he says. "Go. Go. Go."

I put my lips to hers. There is a mismatch. My pencil-thin ones against her cigar-like fleshy ones. I feel the accident of our tongues touching, and I recoil. I suck in, and I blow out not knowing at all what I am doing. My prayers have not stopped shouting in my head. *Please, please, please.*

The man whispers, "in and out, in and out, like a drum-beat."

My own heart is racing. I can't seem to breathe deeply enough. I should have watched those TV dramas more closely.

"Stop," he says, finally.

I come up for air. He thumps on her chest. Up and down. Long black hair bounces on his shoulders. He is lithe and strong.

"Damn city," someone in the crowd says. "Damn EMTs. Where the hell are they when you need them?"

And then, it's like the lights coming back on after a blackout, the sudden surge of power after the city has gone dark. She comes back into her body, her chest heaves ever so slightly. The crowd hoorays and claps like we are at a baseball game, and the batter has hit a home run.

I am overwhelmed with gratitude. The fire of life restored. So this is what it feels like to have your prayers answered. Powerful, humble, searing, freezing. Heat rushes through my body. I'm shaking. We hear the whoo whoo of the ambulance coming down the avenue.

The ambulance arrives with two emergency medical people, and they push everyone out of the way, including me. They set to work with all their gear. Oxygen mask. Monitors. Syringes. They radio the hospital.

"Good work," they bark.

I stand shaking. Can't stop shaking.

The man, my teammate, takes my hands into his and holds them. "Thank you," I whisper, and when I look at him, I am again struck by the odd smoothness of his skin, and I can't place what his ethnicity might be, Indian or Hispanic or maybe a Pacific Islander. He has no facial hair and no wrinkles and no sweat on his brow.

He looks at me, too, not like a stranger, but someone who has known me all my life. "You will be alright," he says calmly, confidently, in a deep, husky voice, that if I weren't married, I might admit was sexy.

"Okay," I say, believing him, but I can't stop shaking. There are probably other, more qualified souls who should have breathed into Jangles, and I don't know why it happened to be me.

They get her big body on the stretcher with the help of my teammate and the bulldog man, who has finally stepped in to help, and strap her down with an oxygen mask and other monitors and tubes, and off she goes into the ambulance, and I want to reach out and touch her one more time. I feel like she has entered me secretly. Because of course I hold her breath in me, and she holds mine.

I look at all her wares spread out on the cardboard, now left abandoned on the street. There are two big shopping bags next to her chair. I start to load the stuff into them when the shopkeeper from the corner store walks over and helps me. He tells me he will keep her stuff safe in his store until she returns.

The crowd disperses, and I look for the man; I want to thank him again, or at least say goodbye, but I can't spot him in the crowd, and I don't see his back or his baseball-capped head bobbing away down the street. He's disappeared. I feel let down. I don't want to be left alone. I want him to tell me one more time that I will be okay, even if it wasn't me who went down on the street, because when he said it to me the first time, I felt, well, *loved*.

3

I hope Zoo will have beaten me home, but it's wishful thinking. The apartment is hot and stuffy and glum. I open all the windows wide to let in whatever breeze might wander our way. I call him at work, but Sunday Smith, his secretary, tells me he's in a meeting.

"Can you have him call me when he gets out?" I hate the way I sound so meek, as if I have to beg to have my own husband call me.

"Got it," she tells me in her super-efficient, sweet-but-laced-with-artificial-sweetener, "I'm too busy for you" style.

Around me are the furnishings Zoo and I had carefully selected when we set ourselves up in the small co-op-owned apartment bought on the promise of Zoo's bright career. There is the plush wool area rug, the custom-made sectional sofa covered in nubby forest-green tricot, the handblown glass pendant lamp, the fireplace with its elegant deco screen, and the formal dining table that sits in the small space next to the kitchen. It's an old building and repairs to plumbing and heating are routinely required, and plaster dust wafts down every time a heavy truck goes by four stories below.

I'm still shaking. I should work while I wait for him, but I go to our bedroom and lower the shades blocking out the view of the stoic branches of the maple tree, which will enliven us with shades of red and orange in another month or two, then go bare, succumbing to winter. Thinking of winter makes me feel an unnamable sadness. I crawl under the thin cotton coverlet. I feel exhausted and wouldn't mind the onset of winter if it meant I could hibernate.

When I wake up I'm startled by the deep shadows in the room and the dead quiet of the apartment. It feels like the middle of the night. How long have I slept? The clock tells me it's only eight. I call out Zoo's name, thinking he must be home by now. I lift myself out of bed, oddly heavy. What was I dreaming? I can't remember, but Jangles' motionless body haunts me. The sound of an ambulance siren careens from one end of the room to the other. I wonder if Jangles will live. The look in the man's eyes still stirs in me. If she survived, it was because of him.

I get out of bed to make dinner. There is late summer light in the sky. I try Zoo's cell, but he doesn't pick up. He can't still be in the meeting. I leave a message that's half-angry, half-pleading. I rinse and moisten the rice flakes until they are soft and al dente. I chop sweet purple onions and cilantro leaves. The knife thudding against the cutting board over and over calms me. I mix in yogurt and cumin seeds crushed in my palms. Cooking, food, nourishment—it's how we came together. Now it doesn't seem to be enough. Now we always seem to be drowning our appetites in shoulds and should nots.

I met Zoo at a party, Upper East Side, summertime, barbecue ribs, pale ale. Nita, my little sister, took me, and it was more her crowd than mine. Business types, accountants and stockbrokers and bond traders. Zoo and I found ourselves alone on a skinny balcony facing the alley. He said he pined for some good Indian food—you can get the best Indian cooking in London, you know, and I said, well I can cook better. He raised an eyebrow.

"I might take you up on that," he said.

"Go ahead."

He called a day later. Nita was huffy, and I said, feel free, have him, but she declined. She was just acting jealous. Niles Worthington (his real name) is husband material, she said, your market, not mine. How do you know, I asked, and she said she checked up on him. London born and raised, Harvard M.B.A., fancy Wall Street firm, no girlfriend, nice apartment, worked hard, hardly played. So I had him over with my university crowd, intellectual types, and cooked a spectacular seven-course Indian meal, home-cooked dishes you can't get in any restaurant, like stuffed bitter melon and chutney from squash skin. He swooned.

"I concede," he said. "Better than London."

He charmed everyone with naughty tales of the business world, celebrity clients, and tragic stock declines. I liked his ability to meld and also the way, when he said goodbye, the last to leave that evening, his kiss was brief and shy. He poked me in a rib and said he found me dangerous.

"Food is my weakness," he said.

"I have other talents, you know, besides cooking."

"Oh yeah, what?"

"You'll have to find out, won't you?"

"That I will," he said. And he did.

Now I wonder where all that cheek came from. Another hour ticks away. No Zoo. No key turning in the lock first to the left, then two turns to the right. He's always working. Complaining about a workaholic husband in this economy would only make me seem like a spoiled brat. Still, the loneliness takes residence like mold that's found a wet and warm place. He won me, and now he's losing me. Or did I win him? When all is said and done, you really can win a man through his stomach. How a man wins a woman is an entirely different question.

I call my parents. When your life's work involves sitting all day in a small office translating texts written in Sanskrit, the ancient classical language, there isn't much to gossip about, so I'm excited to have a real-life story to tell.

My mother, from the safety of her suburban Chicago house, does not like the sound of my adventure on Amsterdam Avenue. I can hear the shopping channel playing on the television in the background. I have given her too many details, a mistake. I told her how Jangles is always on the street corner.

"Who is the woman?" she wants to know. "What do you mean she sells things on the street? What kind of things? Do you need to be checked by a doctor?"

"She's the one who had the heart attack."

Papa, who is a radiologist takes the phone, and wants to hear all the details. He says I am a damn fool to exchange spit with a stranger. He shortlists all the diseases transmitted by spit:

TB, polio, mononucleosis, influenza, herpes, and hepatitis B.

I cut him off. "What if it was you dying on the street? Wouldn't you want someone like me to help you? And isn't this how you get points in heaven? Doing good?"

"You are too young to worry about all that," he says, his voice gravelly from childhood asthma. But he has always lectured us about doing *puñas,* good deeds. How many times did he pontificate to Nita and me about the Hindu way? His favorite line was "Do you want to be reborn as a cockroach?" He tried so hard to instill in us the deeper lessons of karma and dharma, fate and duty. Together, as a family, we watched the serialization of the *Mahabharata* and the *Ramayana,* the two famous books of Hindu lore, on VHS. Of the two daughters, I was the better student. Papa instructed me early in Sanskrit. In high school, he engaged me in philosophical discussions about the journey of the soul, most of which went right over my head. Still, I earned the stripes of the good daughter. Nita cleverly found escape in other activities: tennis, drama club, boys.

Mama and Papa, off the boat for twenty-eight years, American citizens for fifteen, Republicans for longer than that, and still only a heartbeat away from the land of rice and dal.

"She listens to Christian radio, for god's sake," I tell my father.

He is not convinced. He wants to know when I am coming home for a visit. He tells me he misses me.

"I miss you too, Papa," I say.

He hands the phone back to Mama. She wants to know what Zoo and I ate for dinner. She wants to know what I cooked for him. So I have to tell her he isn't home; he's working late.

"Again?" She asks, echoing, of course, my own thoughts.

"Yes, Mama, again. But I made *poha*."

"Only that?"

"He doesn't like to eat heavy."

"But so little?"

"There's bread and cheese and olives, too."

"This is lunch," she says. "You ate without him?"

"No, I am not eating without him. I'm waiting." I sigh. No good Indian woman eats before her husband.

She wants to know if I have spoken with Nita, who is now living in Atlanta.

"She has a new boyfriend," my mother tells me.

"Who is he?"

"How do I know? She only tells me so much."

"I'll call her." My parents' disappointment with Nita is palpable. She's twenty-nine-years old, and there is no husband on the horizon. Surprisingly they have come to approve of Zoo even though he is not Indian. He is a good wage earner, and he treats them with respect.

I hang up with my parents and call Nita right away. She tells me she is on her way out the door and can't talk for long so I tell her the story of Jangles in brief.

"Shit like that happens for a reason," she says wisely.

"Okay, little sis," I say. "So who's the new boyfriend?"

"Can't talk about it. Don't want to jinx it."

When I hang up with Nita, I confront again the emptiness of the apartment. I put some music on and settle into the sofa with my work. When Zoo doesn't come home by nine, then nine-thirty, then almost ten, I try not to think of him having a heart attack on the street or whatever weird misfortune may have befallen him. A hit and run. A subway crash. A mugging. And then I catch myself thinking if I were a bereaved widow I would have a good reason not to finish my Ph.D. Stop, I scream at myself.

But if nothing has happened to him, and he just hasn't bothered to call, then I'm really angry. But that's not like him either. I try to maintain focus on the translations in front of me. The ancient texts tell us over and over to learn to endure all that is fleeting, finite, here today, gone tomorrow. Focus on the infinite, the eternal—love, knowledge, god. Like an idiot, I'm still learning.

And then the familiar key-turn in the lock. He stops at the door to remove his shoes.

"Sorry, baby," he says, padding over to me in socks.

"It's after ten," I say.

"I know, I know. Ed begged me to go have a beer. Problems at home."

Ed is Zoo's colleague and best friend. Mary is Ed's Filipino wife, and the four of us often go out and explore ethnic cuisine together: Vietnamese and Uzbekistani and Ethiopian.

Zoo encircles me lightly with his arms and delivers a kiss to the top of my head. He plops down next to me on the sofa, shoving all my books and papers to the side. I pull away.

"Don't be angry," he says. He yanks his shirttails from his cinched waist and loosens his tie and his belt and wiggles his toes and sheds his day on Wall Street.

I look into his face, into the weariness of his steadfast russet eyes, the latent stubble of the morning's shave, the familiar but not unattractive knob at the end of his nose, the perfectly round chin that I always want to bite.

"You could have called. Did Sunday give you my message? Didn't you get the message I left?"

"I didn't get a message."

"Why doesn't she ever give you my messages?"

"She hates wives."

"Great. Nice."

Zoo breaks away to fish around in the kitchen to see what's for dinner. I follow him in. Zoo helps himself to a spoonful of *poha*.

"Yummy," he says. "Have you eaten?"

I shake my head.

"You waited for me?"

"I did."

"So then let's eat," he says cheerfully.

Zoo sets two places at the table. He brings over the food.

"Are you going to join me for dinner, or are you going to sulk?" he asks.

I'm standing in limbo between the kitchen and the dining-room table. "I'm not sulking. I'm brooding."

"Ahh."

"Come brood over here." He takes my hand and leads me to the table.

"Just call next time. Is that too much to ask?"

"No, not at all. I apologize."

We sit at the table.

"What's wrong with Ed and Mary?"

"The usual. He's always working; she's always partying."

"Well at least she doesn't sit around waiting for him like a good little wife."

Zoo looks up and pauses. "I said I was sorry. You shouldn't have waited for me to eat."

I have to drop it. He has apologized at least three times. Our spoons clink against our bowls as we eat.

"I think I saw Shiva today."

"Who's that?" Zoo says as he shovels another spoon of the *poha* into his mouth, thinking, I guess, that I mean a friend or colleague or relative.

"The god."

"O…kay."

I tell him what happened. He knows of Jangles because she is an Upper West Side fixture, always at the same street corner selling her wares.

"I've never been that close to someone dying," I say. "I prayed for her to live."

"I hope you didn't pray to my god, because I never got anything I prayed for."

"The weird thing is I think he showed up. In the flesh."

"Who?"

"Shiva!"

"O…kay. Are you okay?"

"I mean nobody would help. Nobody. People stood around watching, and nobody did anything. It was disgusting. And all I could do was hold her hand. I was useless. Then this man finally comes over. Actually he kind of floated over. I can't describe it. And he smelled like the flowers my grandmother used to have at her altar. This was just after I had prayed for Jangles to live or maybe I was still praying. I don't know. Actually I was begging. *Let her live.* And he whispers to me to do the mouth-to-mouth thing. And I do it. But he doesn't look like a real man. He has no hair on his face, no wrinkles, no pockmarks. He's beautiful to look at."

"Are you sure it was a man—"

"Yes, I'm sure. He was wearing a blue cap and a blue T-shirt."

"What is your point?"

"I'm telling you he wasn't like any other person I've ever met. And he did save her life. I'm convinced of it. Whatever he did, it was magic."

"I think he did what you're supposed to do when someone has a heart attack."

I look angrily at Zoo. I don't want his rational explanations. "Yes, but it was more than that. I felt all this heat, all this energy pour out of him. And then she just popped back to life."

"Okay. So you saw god. Big deal. Can we talk about something else? You're scaring me. You should see your face. You look possessed."

"What do you want to talk about? The stock market?" I've gotten loud and angry and sarcastic.

"Oh my god. I'm sorry if I don't believe gods just come down to earth and show up in blue caps and blue T-shirts."

"What *do* you believe in?"

Zoo stands up abruptly and clears his bowl off the table. "I'm tired. Long day."

I look into my bowl. Flecks of turmeric-yellowed rice flakes dotted with chopped green cilantro stare back at me. I've worked myself up into a state of confusion, annoyance, even rage. I was never someone who just picked a fight with my husband. I've always hated that. But here I am. Changing into that. Of course I didn't see *him*. Why does the man haunt me then? He appeared and disappeared, like the sun playing behind a cloud.

4

onday morning, a light drizzle sweetens the air as I walk to my office. I approach 96th and Amsterdam, and there's a crack of thunder. The drizzle turns to a hard rain. I crowd into the canopied entryway of a shoe store, caught without an umbrella, and watch with the others as rain hammers the sidewalk. There is no sign of Jangles. The corner seems a blank now, like when a song stops playing on the radio, but the music is still with you.

As soon as the rain lets up, I run out and up the four blocks to the university. Zoo has Wall Street; I have my den at Columbia U, dust laden and graced with a slab of filtered noonday sun. Not every Ph.D. hopeful has this. I seem to breathe easier as soon as I'm here, despite the dank air and the clutter. A note is taped to the door of my office. The familiar handwriting of my boss, Dr. Ellen Dickey, Sanskrit scholar, Chair of the Department of World Religions. I call her Duck. She wants to see me as soon as I get in. Duck has hired me, classical Sanskrit scholar, (thank you, Papa, for my early start) to help her tackle words written thousands of years ago. She says my Sanskrit is better than hers.

I feel nervous walking down the hall and up the flight of stairs to her office. My feet squelch in my shoes. What could it be? Is she going to fire me? It is true I've been late on a couple translations, and the end of my marathon run for the Ph.D. is nowhere in sight. I hear voices in her office, and I can see the shadowy out-of-focus figure of someone through the old mottled glass of her office door. I knock tepidly. The door opens, and it is Vanderoe. My stomach lurches. Duck is sitting at her desk. I would have much preferred Duck to be my adviser, but the department wouldn't allow it because I work for her. Too much of a conflict of interest. They both look at me in a way that suggests that I might have been the subject of their conversation.

"Do you want to tell her, or should I?" Duck asks Vanderoe.

"Go ahead," Vanderoe says. "It's your party."

"We got the grant!" Duck says, and she's out of her chair and sashaying her hips and waving her arms in the air and jumping up and down like a prizewinning contestant on television. This is why I love her.

"Wow. That's fantastic." I hug her. I wonder if Vanderoe isn't a little bit jealous. They have an old rivalry. The grant means Duck will be able to finish her book and continue to pay me, I hope.

I love Duck because she's been around a long time, she knows the academic world, and she knows Sanskrit and Greek and Latin and Pali and has also dabbled in ancient Egyptian. She loves the ancient world the way people love their children.

She could care less about the inequality of the pay scale at the university (the students have taken up the cause of the janitorial staff), or the failure of the world market, or the negligent stewardship of the earth. She's only interested in cutting a wide swath through ancient thinking. She's drawn to language and meaning, and she is a fantastic teacher because she makes the old words come to life as if they were written yesterday. She would like people to know that Hinduism is not just about day-glo gods prancing about on lions with more arms and legs than octopi. She has even made a style out of her quilted wool skirts and heavy tights and bright red sweaters and neck scarves and French berets. She waddles, which is why I call her Duck.

Dr. Hugh Vanderoe is another beast altogether. His unbridled passion is solely for himself. Duck suggests we go out to lunch and celebrate. She leans back in her chair, rests her hands on the top of her head, and scolds me with her eyes.

"This is important work, you know. This is going to reach way beyond academia." The book is a new translation and interpretation of the seminal Vedic texts.

Vanderoe says he has a meeting with the dean and won't be able to make lunch.

"Still trying to get my job?" Duck says mischievously.

"No, actually, I'm trying to get his job," Vanderoe says.

We all laugh. Someday I too am supposed to learn how to navigate the treacherous, political waters of academia.

"Ellen and I were just discussing the progress of your thesis," Vanderoe says.

I feel my heart muscle tighten up, my jaw clench.

"I've scheduled you to defend by next May." He has significant eyebrows and a famous patrician nose, but it is his height and the assuming way he cocks his head that is intimidating. When he talks, he intones. He stands over me by a good eight inches. "Is there any reason you can't meet that deadline?" he asks.

I had planned on a July defense, but I know there is no excuse under the sun that would sound anything other than lame, and nine more months following on four years is more of a gift than a deadline.

"I can. I think I can."

"You think or you will? Commit. It's the only way."

"Yes, Hugh is right," Duck says.

"I commit," I say.

The subject of my Ph.D. is mysticism and literature and religious belief as revealed through the life and writings of the mystic Virashaiva poets and saints of South India from the twelfth century. Shiva worshippers. I must illuminate the poetry of mysticism and the worldview of the Virashaiva saints (heretical) and also make a mark on the study of religious literature. Vanderoe, Greek and Byzantine scholar, says that a Ph.D. that simply illuminates a group of poets is not going to be sufficient. I must put them in the context of soteriological theory and modern scholarly thinking about mysticism. I must give scientific data and use methodological reasoning.

Vanderoe tells me he wants to see an action plan on his desk by the afternoon. He wants to see the introduction next week and chapters on a regular basis. I nod. Of course, of course.

"Do it," Duck says. "I can up you on the grant if you have your doctorate."

"Done," I say, as much to convince myself. During the past four years, others have mastered brain surgery and aced the bar exam, and I'm still wrestling with a bunch of poets. Maybe I love my work too much, maybe that's my problem. I don't want to leave it behind.

"I need those translations," Duck says. "This last set was excellent. You do have a way with the language."

I bask in her praise. It's nice to have Vanderoe hear it, too. I pause at the door before leaving to tell them about my rescue operation on the street, although I can hear in my voice that the story is getting worn. The details have turned a little pale in the re-enactment. I mention how I prayed to Shiva. I know Duck at least will find it interesting.

"Imagine a statistical analysis of how many prayers have been offered and how many have actually been answered. Now that would be worthy of a big fat grant," Vanderoe says.

"Shiva's not a bad choice," Duck says. "God of life and death. But maybe he loves death a little too much."

I want to tell her no, not in this case, I don't believe so; I think he stepped in on the side of life, but she lowers her glasses on her nose and squints up at her computer screen, which has just dinged to let her know an email has come in.

5

ack in my office, I take one look and wince. Books are piled alongside my computer, various incarnations of thesis chapters everywhere, notes on notes taped on the walls, even more books to wade through on the floor, cases of water, heavy Icelandic wool sweaters left from last winter because the heat never works in here, two old computers waiting to go to repair, a gym bag, the ancient file cabinet that doesn't close properly. The walls are equally crammed—I collect the day-glo imagery of the Indian gods that Duck hates. There are glossy color posters of Shiva and his equally potent wife, Parvati; Ganesha, the elephant-headed god, who I should be praying to now to remove all obstacles from finishing my Ph.D.; Krishna, the Hindu Apollo; Saraswati, goddess to those who love art and music and learning; and Lakshmi, for those who want wealth and good fortune. I love their pale blue skin, the mark of their divinity, and the way they are decked out with flower garlands and jewels and golden crowns. I stare into Shiva's eyes, wondering what I will find there. A resemblance, maybe, to the man in the baseball cap? Yes, I see it. The long eyelashes. The preternaturally smooth skin. The long, black hair. I look away quickly. What silliness. Zoo is right.

I dump books out of my desk chair. I want to work at home where this kind of chaos is not allowed. The phone rings. It's Nita, weepy and miserable. She tells me that her new boyfriend has just dumped her.

"Why?" I ask.

"He's seeing someone else."

"Oh, Nita." My heart drops for her. "Do you know who?"

She sniffles. "She's this beautiful half-Asian, half-Irish copy editor. She's a biker and a dancer."

"Christ."

"And she has big boobs."

"She sounds very shallow."

"Wading-pool shallow," Nita says.

"Maybe it was time to move on," I say gently.

"Move on! I hadn't even moved in," she says.

"Love is messy. That's all I can say." I feel a dull muddy cloud gather in my head and chest. I tell her I have to get back to work and promise to call her over the weekend.

I click on the chapter titled "The Divine Lover." It's where I left off last week. It is a small chapter buried in my thesis about the young saint and mystic poet Akka Mahadevi. *Akka* means big sister; *Mahadevi* means huge goddess. But she was not a goddess, just a young girl infatuated with god. With Shiva. In fact it was her I was thinking about when I was walking home and encountered Jangles. She has given me so many problems, this little saint. Her story is peculiar. She wasn't after social reform, just love. I first heard of her story from my father who had grown up with tales of the saints' lives and learned their poetry. His native tongue, *Kannada*, was theirs. But of all the saints, Akka Mahadevi was one of the most beloved. Vanderoe would probably have me cut this chapter from the thesis, but I feel an odd attachment to her, probably because my father always spoke so affectionately about her.

She was born in the dust of South India to a farmer and his back-bent wife, thin and threadbare folk, living off the scarce bounty of the land. At ten, she found a guru who initiated her into Shiva worship. Creator, Destroyer. God with eighty-four-hundred-thousand faces. God with one-thousand-and-eight names. The cosmic dancer. It was a fateful encounter.

But when she was just twelve, a local feudal chieftain, King Kausika, saw her and fell for her. She already had a reputation as a village beauty. He wanted to marry her. Powerless and penniless, her parents could not refuse. Akka was handed over. A bride at thirteen, she became Kausika's royal queen. She was forced to fulfill all that was asked of her in the earthly world of husbands and palaces. Lie in his royal bed, as the story goes.

But what of Shiva, her true love? She refused to give him up. She spent hours in the temple praying to her true lord. Kausika, jealous husband, demanded she choose. He would not share his bed. Me or him.

Him.

Akka seized the moment and ran from the palace. All

of sixteen now, she abandoned village and home, mother and father. Wandered barefoot. Naked. Naked! Dressed only in the covering of her long, black hair. Scorned. Defiant. Disgraced. That's when she wrote her love poems. Her name for Shiva was *My Lord White as Jasmine*.

Vanderoe's not interested in love poetry. He wants facts and analysis and how they lead to social transformation. I pick up Akka's poems again. Scan them for anti-societal tracts.

> *One husband for this life*
> *And one for the other?*
> *One for the body*
> *And one for the spirit*
> > *I have my lord white as jasmine*
> *All other husbands are but*
> *Painted puppets*
> *Hiding in shadows!*

I start typing away on my computer, retooling the chapter. There was no feminist movement to argue against child marriage, no one to root for a teenage girl who simply would not obey the rules. Who does she turn to? One of the most powerful gods in the pantheon: Shiva. Shiva who can reduce Kama, the god of love, to ashes. Shiva who swallows an ocean of poison in order to save the world and in so doing gains nothing more than a blue stain on his neck. Shiva who breaks the anger of Ganga, the river goddess, with his head and takes her for his second wife, saving the earth from deluge. If Akka can get Shiva to take her as his bride, she will be liberated from those who would have her soul caged by a feudal king, spared from the constant ballooning of her womb with countless suckling children, left to grow withered and old in the tides of desert sand. So she sets off on a journey of her own making, bold, young thing, blessed with the gift of verse. It is a story of pure love but also a story of rebellion. I read Akka's other poems. I rest on one.

> *I'm turned upside down*
> *The breeze is on fire*
> *The moonlight burns me like a hot sun*
>
> *Like the tax collector,*
> *My work is never ending*
>
> *Please, friend, let Him know*
>
> *Bring Him here*
> *My lord white as jasmine*
>
> *He is angry*
> *That we are two*

A sudden heat rises in me as I read the poem. The fire of her sexual longing. What is the boundary between what the heart desires and what the body desires? The male poets don't write of sexual love, of course. That is what makes her different, important.

The lively eyes, the lithe body of the blue-capped man comes to me. I feel Akka's thirst inside me. A mystery to me, that love of the divine. A puzzle I will have to solve if I ever hope to finish this thing. I feel the warm breath of his eyes again. And then I feel immediate shame, guilt. The twelfth century seems not so long ago.

6

Frisbee players are out on the quad, and bikini-clad girls are pulling their jeans on as the afternoon sun loses its heat. I'm packing it in for the day, although I don't want to. I shouldn't. We are meeting Zoo's parents for dinner. They are passing through town on their way from London to Los Angeles. I've hardly made a dent in the translations I owe Duck, so I load them in my bag and vow to get to them in the evening. Begging out of dinner would look bad; it's not as if we see Roger and Mimi that often. They are sensitive about imposing on us; they would never dream of staying with us in our apartment, or calling us up at the last minute. Visits get planned months ahead of time. They are the exact opposite of my parents who would be mortified to stay in a hotel when their child has a perfectly decent apartment in town.

Akka tosses in my mind; I can't shake the image of her young, calloused feet treading the continent in search of her divine lover. Imagine me wandering naked through Manhattan with only my tresses to cover me, reciting love poems to Shiva. They would cart me off to Bellevue in less time than it would take to buy a subway token.

A quick shower at home, and I put on a nice skirt and blouse and head downtown. The temperature drops as I step into the restaurant, and my eyes have to adjust to the darkness of spot lighting and plush red carpet. I should have taken a cab because the subway has made me hot and sweaty and choked. I tell the host I'm meeting people, and I peer past him, but the tall paneled booths keep everyone's privacy in tact. Niles Worthington, I tell him. And he looks down on his list, and yes, they are already here, and he leads me to the booth.

Roger stands to greet me, towering above me, broad-shouldered, lean, a bit red in the face and short in the neck. I lean over and give Mimi a peck on the cheek and get a nice whiff of a lavender fragrance. My butt sticks as I try to slide into the leather seat next to Zoo.

"You look lovely, darling," Mimi says. Her eyes are bright and energetic. "We were just talking about how it's been ridiculously long since we've seen you both."

"Yes, it's been far too long," Roger says, smiling.

"That's because you guys are too busy to visit us," I tease.

"We have been awfully busy," Mimi says. "I had the most dreadful deadline on my book. The editor was breathing down my neck every day."

"I'm in the same situation," I say. "My adviser's given me a strict deadline of May 1st for my thesis. Otherwise I'm cooked."

Zoo lifts his wineglass. "To deadlines," he says. "To Anjali finishing her thesis and us getting on with our life."

"It's not that bad," I say defensively. "You're the one who's stuck in the office every night until nine."

"No one can afford to sit on their ass in this economy," Roger says with his eyebrows raised. He is a devoted businessman, a man who has enjoyed a long and successful career in diamonds and understands the vagaries of the market.

"Come with me to the Brooklyn Botanical tomorrow," Mimi says. "They are having a special exhibit on native plants of the Eastern Seaboard." Mimi is a horticulturalist. She has an extensive background in native plants and has published two books already. When I visited London with Zoo, just after we were engaged, she took me on an exhaustive garden tour of the city.

Mimi tells us she is in a pitched battle with her local horticultural club. She has formed a Native Plant Society for London.

"They hate me," she says, "because I detest their precious cottage gardens. But the up-and-coming landscape designers are completely on board."

"If anyone can change those asses, you can, darling," Roger says.

"Oh, but they'll persist, won't they? I live and long for the native rolling heathers and heaths of the countryside. We need to preserve the native English landscape." Her face is alive and impassioned. "This is why I'm so excited to see the exhibit tomorrow. Apparently the fungus *Discula destructiva* has completely threatened the *Cornus florida*, all your eastern dogwoods. What a shame."

When I toured the London gardens with Mimi I almost

came to resent, as she did, those nasty non-native invaders—the tulips from Turkey and lilies from the Orient—all from the East, until I realized me and my family and all immigrants are just like those plants, nasty foreign intruders.

The talk turns to Zoo's family—his sister and her two boys, Henry and Alexander, and the sleazy, washed-up husband she is in the middle of divorcing.

"Do you know his lawyer is suing for fifty percent of her share in the Worthington Family Trust?"

Zoo raises an eyebrow. "Won't get very far with that—"

"Certainly not," Roger says emphatically. "It's well protected against nasty husbands and wives."

Zoo pokes me in the ribs. "Hear that, darling?"

"I hear," I say. "I know my place in this family."

"Oh, darling, it's not like that at all," Mimi says quickly, embarrassed. "We adore you. And you and Niles make such a wonderful couple. Nothing like that will ever happen to the two of you."

Despite Mimi's reassurances, the comment leaves a sour taste in my mouth. Zoo changes the conversation to work. When he talks about business he gets excited, and his voice jumps an octave. He waves his hands around as if he's a conductor. Something about a company that has gone south. And how others' misfortunes have created great opportunities for those in the right position. Roger is all ears.

I remember one of Akka's lines. *In a garden without soil grows a tree without leaves. Fruit, or no fruit I go there and without chewing, eat it.* I pull a small notepad from my purse and write a note to myself: Akka and metaphysical barrenness?

Mimi looks at her watch and reminds Roger that she has an early wake-up call. She asks me again if she can tempt me to the Brooklyn Botanical, but I beg out, reminding her of my deadline. Zoo signs for dinner on his credit card, and I can tell both he and Roger are pleased; the son is taking them out for dinner; he has made it. We linger on the sidewalk as we wait for cabs, and Zoo and I tuck them safely into the first one that comes along. Another cab comes and we load ourselves in, and I throw my head back on the seat and Zoo checks the messages on his cell phone.

"I don't know how your mother can bear to be in New York City or London, or any city, where everyone and everything is a non-native mishmash of what just landed on the shore, including a bunch of Indians like me."

"You know that isn't what she means at all."

"I'm not sure."

"Silver and Gold merger went through," Zoo says, reading off a text on his phone.

"How can you hate plants, for god's sake? They're so innocent."

"Either a whole bunch of people are going to get laid off or—"

"Or what?"

"Or I don't know. Could be good. Good for me."

"How?"

"Dunno. Yet. Must investigate. I'll tell you what's not innocent. Corporate mergers that happen in the dark of the night." Zoo texts away, his fingers speeding to type out letters.

We pass Central Park. The trees are dark and still. There are plenty of people about, enjoying the cool relief of the evening.

"Let's get out and walk," I suggest to Zoo.

He looks up anxiously from his texting. Sizes up where we are.

"Okay, sure, why not."

So we have the taxi pull over and head up alongside the park. Zoo slips his phone into his pocket and takes my hand.

This is why you get married, I think. For this. For this moment right now. So you can walk hand in hand up a street and feel that the pulsing of the world can't touch you. That two against the world is enough. How sad it would be not to have this. I grip Zoo's hand tighter. Holding on as if he is my anchor, my strength.

7

His hair hangs in long, black ringlets like a woman's and seduces my nipples. Every pore is singing. I feel his desire for me, and that sets me on fire. I am lying on his tiger-skin-covered bed, soft as moss, looking at precious stars in a night sky. A warm breeze teases my hair. The half moon suffuses us in her pale glow and glimmers off his blue-skinned body. There is the perfume of wild fennel and lavender. And coconut? But it is as if a noisy city street is just around the corner, and car honks and brakes screeching jar my ears.

Flames seem to lick my thighs. Two of his hands hold my buttocks entirely, sear me with their heat, and his other two hands rake through my hair. I hold him firmly by his shoulders. I look to his eyes for guidance, clues, but he flutters them closed, and so I close mine. He enters me, and I don't notice until I do. I expand from inside out, like a balloon swelling with helium. We make love like new lovers who are only just beginning to discover the taste, the smell, the curve of the rib of the other. His lips are salty and sweet. His body so easy to hold, to grasp, and incredibly soft and yielding. This, I feel, should never end. We can be here forever, drinking from a spring that will never run dry. I see a giant movie screen and on it is an image of a group of women in saris of all colors singing and dancing in a meadow full of flowers. Then an image of men opposite the women, also singing and dancing. There are drums and trumpets and a huge symphonic score that feels like it is going to swallow us up. So this is all a movie I think. What fun.

And then we are in a car driving somewhere, except we are going backwards. In reverse. Mountain roads with hairpin curves—I am at the wheel and the windows are wide open, and the wind is whipping through my hair. For some reason the wind does nothing to his hair. He tells me I'm a good driver. I ask him where we are going.

And then we are back on the tiger skin making delicious love. Are we on top of the car as it is going backwards? Who is driving?

He speaks. His voice is as thick and luscious as mango pulp. *I want to see if you are the one.*

I look at him curiously. Why, I wonder. Why me?

And just like that he disappears, and the dream is over.

Zoo is already out of bed and logged on to his computer when I turn to face him at seven in the morning. I feel a sinking sense as if I've done something wrong, but what? And then the dream comes back. Am I losing it? Sly devil, he came to me in a dream. Two legs, sculpted torso, four arms? Four long arms! He appeared at the foot of my bed as if he had been re-materialized by a Star Trek transporter, whole and breathing, more human than god. He held his hand out for mine, beckoning. *Come,* he said. *Come on. What are you afraid of? We are just going to play.*

Zoo is rubbing his neck, always knotted and tight. His knee is jogging in place. He slams the cover of his laptop shut. He disappears into the bathroom and reappears a few minutes later, emerging with his face lathered and readied for morning scraping.

"Everything okay?" I ask.

"My stock picks are going down. Everyone is going to be feasting off my dead carcass." He looks ghostly with his half-white face. He disappears into the bathroom again.

When he comes back into the bedroom, I tell him I'm sorry.

"Stocks go up. Stocks go down."

How do you apologize for a dream? I go over to him and massage his neck and shoulders. He relaxes into my fingers.

"You got something to wear for the twelfth?"

"What's on the twelfth?" I ask.

"The thing. The party. The merger. Silver & Silver. Getting Gold Group."

"What day of the week is that?"

"Thursday."

"I can't go. That's the opening day of the conference."

"What conference?"

"The one we're hosting with Modern Languages."

"You've got to be at this party. It's the biggest thing of the year."

"Zoo, I can't. I'm sure the big reception is that evening. It's been on my calendar for months. You didn't tell me about this party."

He drops his pajamas and pulls on underwear and socks. He shuffles through his clothes on the rod and starts to whistle. He pushes clothes around back and forth in the closet. "We can't look shabby. We need to go shopping."

"I really can't get out of the conference."

Zoo turns and looks at me. "You've got to. I'm going to need you there. They're talking promotions. They're talking layoffs."

"So what's my presence going to change?"

"Silver likes stability. He likes people who are going to stick around. Married couples. People with kids, families."

"Gee, maybe we can borrow a couple kids off the street," I say.

"Darling, you've got to do this for me. Please. Don't abandon me." Zoo's eyes bear down on me; his expression is serious, almost desperate. "I need this promotion. This is the company to be with right now."

Duck's disapproval plays in my mind. Vanderoe's disgust. Would Zoo give up something equally important for me?

Zoo pulls at his midline. "Fuck, I think I'm gaining weight. Look." And he pulls again on his side just above his hip and pinches a mound of flesh between his fingers. "You're getting fat, too," he says. "No more Indian food."

I don't say anything. I drop back onto the bed. Close my eyes. *He* comes back. So blue. The memory brings an awkward tingling between my legs. *His* eyes. Lovely. Wait. My eyes pop open. The same eyes as the man who helped with Jangles. I get out of bed. My heart races.

Zoo puts on a white shirt. A chalky gray silk tie. A lightweight, well-cut suit jacket. He checks his face in the mirror for nicks or bits of lather.

I walk into the kitchen to cut fruit and pour Zoo his bowl of cereal and make myself a cup of tea. Morning light blasts its way in.

Zoo sets his briefcase on the kitchen table and pours milk over his fruit and cereal. Takes a couple bites. Leaves the rest. He checks in his briefcase for his laptop, pens, and keys.

I take his cereal bowl and put it in the sink. I feel anger rising. "I'm working late tonight. Get yourself dinner," I tell him.

"Will do. Lucky me. Off to prison I go."

"Then why do you love it so?"

"Ha ha, make a rhyme of it. Very clever. Who do you know who loves having their head under a guillotine every minute of the day never knowing when the damn thing's going to fall and send your head rolling?"

"You."

"Let's just hope it's a promotion. Okay? Then we're home free."

The door clicks shut. I repeat the words. "Home free." I drop onto the sofa. Shaken up by a feeling of impending doom. But nothing has happened. My feet twitch nervously. I can't get the breath in deep enough. An anxiety attack. The dream. He wants to see if I am the one. I laugh. Akka, I have met your lover. Again? I fish into my book bag and find the sheaf of her poems.

I know there is one where she describes him.

I have seen him,

Fourteen worlds blaze with his light.

His shining hair, red in the sun
And beautiful teeth, white and gleaming
And his crown of rubies

How he laughs!

The lover I met had the whitest teeth I have ever seen. Were they pearls? And hair that tumbled over his shoulders like a waterfall. Skin that was silky and blue. Long, tapered finger- nails that aroused little moans as they made their way up the sides of me. I blush, remembering it.

I have seen him, the Great One, and lost my hunger

He is the master and
Even men are his wives!

I have seen him,
who is playmate to Shakti
My lord white as jasmine

Now I have been born!

I finish my morning cup of tea. Dress for work. Organize my papers. She lost her hunger. When will I lose mine?

8

J angles is back! It has been more than two weeks. She
looks less queenly than she used to, holding her arms at the
elbows, rocking. She wears her turban and a thick wool
coat even though it is a warm September day. I walk up to her.
I look over the cardboard and all the stuff on it, her usual wares,
pretending to be interested in an alarm clock. She looks at me.
I smile stupidly.

"Winter's coming," she says, holding up a turquoise blue
scarf, her eyes asking if I might like to make a purchase. I take it
from her, turn it over, its fibers soft and comforting in my palm.
There is no sign of recognition from her.

"How are you feeling?" I ask.

Now she looks at me. "The good Lord looks out after
me," she says.

"I was here the day you had the heart attack."

"You were the one?"

"Yes, and there was someone else, a man. He knew what
he was doing. I was just helping."

"I'll be." A huge smile breaks on her face as she pulls

herself out of her folding lawn chair. All of a sudden I find myself held, the thick pungent smell of perfumed oils washing over me in a wave. "I thought God had elected me," she said. "I surely did."

"Are you well now?" I ask.

She pounds her fist against her heart. Her face is full of color, and her two cheeks, round like hard candy, seem to glow with health.

"You take that scarf. That's from me." She takes the scarf and wraps it around my neck. It's so long it goes around two times with long tails still draping on either side.

"No," I laugh. It's a fake kind of embarrassed laugh I inherited from my mother. "You don't need to do that."

Her eyes bug out. "Are you going to hurt my feelings?"

So I clasp the blue scarf. This, the only scarf she had to sell, and it is the exact color of *his* skin.

9

I tread lightly down the halls of the Humanities building where the World Religions department is housed like an orphan. It is one of the older buildings on campus—heavy stone, worn linoleum floors, feeble lighting. I have always enjoyed the dark and weighty atmosphere of these halls. I pass through the worn wooden doors with their thick, old glass windows, behind which all kinds of serious and ponderous thought have taken place, recorded in books, illuminating the unknown. So much knowledge waiting to be uncovered, contested, refined, and debated. This is something Zoo can't understand, with his preference for all that is real.

On the bulletin board is a large flier for the upcoming conference. Vanderoe's office emits a soft incandescent glow. I tiptoe past it. Stupid of me not to have taken the long way around. I am five steps past the door when he emerges, holding a coffee cup in his hand.

"Ah, it's the holy storyteller. Meet me for lunch. Twelve-thirty." It's part question but mostly command.

I nod meekly.

Safe in my office, I settle at my desk, a bit shaken by the thought of lunch with Vanderoe. He has no doubt read my introduction and wants to discuss it. Will he send me back to the drawing board? I shudder. How many have failed before me? Duck has told me not to worry. He only fails the men, not the women. The women quit when they have their babies and are no threat to him. Or simply end their lives, or try to, like Rebecca. She had had lunch with Vanderoe the day before she did it. I shudder. I make a note to call her.

I call Zoo. "Are you sure I have to be at the Silver and Gold thing?"

"Please, Anjali. This is not a joke."

"She's as strong as a horse," I tell him. I can hear the general chaos of voices behind him in his office that is always the background music of our conversations. He, of course, has no clue what I am talking about. I remind him of Jangles.

"Glad to hear it. Got to go. Over and out."

What is the Sanskrit translation for I love you but I don't have time right now? I finger the blue scarf still wrapped around my neck. Wearing it makes me feel stronger. I take a deep breath and start my day's work. Turn my computer on. Shuffle papers around. He stares at me. Gorgeous. The dream haunts me. Usually my dreams involve missed airplanes and showing up for a lecture without my notes. I email Duck and Vanderoe about the conflict with the party. I'm so contrite that I can't believe they will chastise me too harshly.

At twelve-thirty I knock on Vanderoe's office door. He takes me to the Faculty Club, chastising me on the way for my email. *Going to be missing in action, I see.* We make slow progress to the table. I feel underdressed in jeans and a T-shirt. The blue scarf is a useful distraction. Vanderoe seems to know everyone and works the tables as if it is a wedding or a political gathering. He serves on a lot of university committees. His last book on the science of the religious mind, the key word being *science*, a tome of seven-hundred pages, made a big splash and got a rave notice in the Sunday Book Review.

He orders iced tea and a salad, and I do the same.

He slides over the pages of the introduction I left with him. He had it stuffed and curled in his side pocket. I see his famous vibrant red ink scratches all over the page.

"What's going on here?" he asks.

"I think I finally discovered the heart of my thesis," I say. "It's Akka Mahadevi. She's the link I've been looking for. It's through her story that we really understand the real truth of mystic belief."

"Oh come on, Anjali. Pooh-pooh on little girls who hear voices of gods. We know that story. Tell me something new. Tell me something I don't know."

"Do you really know what it means to give up everything in search of the divine lover?" I ask.

Vanderoe's eyes are full of skepticism. "You need to make a compelling case for why I need to know this. What difference does it make in the world? Build the case for the political rebellion. The direct experience of the divine is a necessary adjustment to the power structure of religion as practiced by the governing priests. Priests want to stand between the devotee and god. They want to regulate the devotee's experience of god and proclaim themselves as the necessary interceder between man and god."

"But Akka Mahadevi's love for Shiva was not an overt political gesture. Yes, she was escaping marital bondage, but for her divine love was real. She saw it as a forbidden love, and her anguish at her separation from him was as real as two lovers who cannot meet. It's the personal aspect of mystic love that draws me to this material."

This causes Vanderoe to raise an eyebrow. "You are more passionate about this now than when you started," Vanderoe eyes me. "Can you maintain a scholarly approach to this?"

"Isn't the best scholarly work informed by passion?"

"There are a lot of passionate crackpot academics. We need to legitimize our work. Use scientific evidence whenever possible. Statistics. How many of these saints were there? Document the repression of the Brahmin priests from available texts. We need to know about the local kings. The strategies of oppression. Analyze her poems scientifically. How many references to god? How many to nature? How many girls her age on the same quest? You get my drift." He waves his fork in the air for emphasis. His eyebrows arch radically upwards; his lips pinch into seriousness. Even sitting down, his height is a problem.

I feel a burning in my chest. I grip my iced tea.

"It's imperative you don't confuse passion with scholarship," he says.

"I know that," I say.

"Good," he says. "Don't get sidetracked. Eat your salad."

10

We are towering over the city on the forty-ninth floor of a Wall Street skyscraper, and to be so high without touching the earth directly scares me. People crowd into the merger party from all sides. I stand close to Zoo and Ed and Mary. Silver and Silver has done reasonably well despite the crash in the economy and the ever-changing world situation. Everyone wants to put on an optimistic veneer on the fear and anger that sits just under their skin. There is an open bar, and a swell develops around it. Zoo greets people in his cheery accent. As promised, all the top brass are in attendance. Zoo and I spent enough on new clothes to supply the neighborhood food pantry with a month's worth of food, but I have to say my new black dress does help me fit in, and Zoo looks sharp in his Italian designer suit. Now we can really play the part of the up-and-coming power couple.

Sunday Smith, Zoo's secretary, walks up to us with a big smile. She's not only the model of efficiency; she has model good looks.

"I love your dress, Angie!" Sunday exclaims.

I cringe the way I do every time she butchers my name.

"Thanks, Sunday," I say, adding my own ration of artificial sweetener.

Damiana Silver, CEO Richard Silver's wife, steps in our direction, and Sunday melts back into the crowd. That is one wife she can't afford to hate. Damiana is all smiles. She radiates a finishing school sort of perfection.

Zoo introduces himself.

"And you must be Mrs. Worthington?" She takes my hand in a thawed-out handshake.

"Anjali," I say, not correcting the last name to Mehta, my maiden name. "A pleasure to meet you."

She inquires as to our summer, how did it go, was it wonderful? Zoo uses the question as an excuse to slip away and talk smart with her husband who is standing only two shoulders away. I tell Damiana we had one lovely week in July in a beach house in Truro. The light is so special on Cape Cod! I hear myself mouthing these words, but the light of the Cape is already a distant memory.

Something is ticking in her eyes. "Are you from India?" she asks.

"Yes, I was born there, but I came to this country when I was six."

"Oh, so you are really American."

"The truth is I'm neither this nor that."

Damiana smiles. "I suppose many Americans feel that way. I certainly do. My father was Irish and my mother Swedish."

Then, surprisingly, she takes my hand into her own. "Richard tells me such super things about your husband. I would love for both of you to join us for supper."

Blood flushes to my face. We have been singled out. "That would be so nice," I murmur. "We would love to have dinner."

"I'll make sure Richard's secretary sets something up," she says and smiles, and I look directly into her eyes and smile, too. And then it's mutually understood that our conversation is over, and she moves on for a visit with the next up-and-coming couple.

Mary grabs me by the arm and nods towards the exit where the restrooms are. She is wearing a lovely green silk suit. It is conservative for her—usually she is in jeans that ride low on her hips and bosom-hugging tank tops.

"What were you guys talking about?" she whispers heavily as we slip out of the room into the quiet hallway.

I tell her we talked about our roots and where we come from.

"Ed better get VP. He got them half their clients."

I am a bit shocked by her boldness. Ed would be mortified to hear Mary say these things.

We walk down the long, empty hall to the restrooms. The click of our heels against the tiled and waxed floors echoes back at us. The offices that line the hall have glass windows, and we can look into them. Some of the desks have neatly stacked papers and computers that have been set to sleep, but others are deserted from all the employees who have been laid off. It feels haunted and spooky down here without anyone around. I could never work in a place like this.

In the bathroom mirror, Mary replenishes her lipstick, an odd orange color that seems to work on her. I redo mine, too. Looking at myself in the mirror, I see the face I know so well, the one I inherited mostly from my father, his dark eyes that question everything, his good straight nose, his high forehead, a forehead that Nita says makes me look more intelligent than I deserve. Jealous little sister. Of course, she got my mother's fair skin and her high cheekbones and her silken hair. My face is one that belongs in the south of India with people who know how to take heat, with goatherds and village dwellers, with Shiva worshippers and mystic poets. What this face is doing at a merger party, trying to impress the wife of the CEO, I cannot figure out. I feel guilty about missing the reception for the conference. There were scholars there I wanted to meet, scholars who have written about mystic cults and the power of the Indian deities. I'm hungry for their knowledge. Anxious to understand the rumblings I've been feeling.

Mary tells me she is studying interior design, and she and Ed are going to redo their apartment. She's going to make it very modern and very hip.

"That's great, Mary," I say. "How is everything going with you two?"

"Sucky." Mary smacks her lips. "We never see each other."

"Wall Street widow," we both say on a bitter note we can't hide.

When we return to the party, we find Zoo and Ed with a small group of colleagues, men and women, all looking sharp and polished. Zoo is telling the story of an on-site visit to a high-tech firm in the Silicon Valley.

"So the owner is showing me around, and it's nothing very impressive, an office building with a warren of dark offices, the usual computer nerds, you know the scene, and a little warehouse out back for manufacturing the samples. And the whole time I'm thinking, I just flew out 3,000 miles for this? You expect me to convince investors to put money into this? I mean I've seen the books, and they're pretty good, but basically the guy has bad breath and is wearing ratty old sneakers and jeans, and he looks like he hasn't had a shave in three, four days. Then we get in his car, and we drive for miles to the middle of nowhere, and he takes me down this unpaved road and walks me into this hangar, not saying a word about what we're about to see."

Everyone listens raptly to Zoo. He's just so with his timing and emphasis. For a moment, I see Zoo in his own light. He is a beautiful creature, freshly born, it seems, tall and immaculate and long-nosed, and his skin breathes out its own sheen like an unblemished and unwaxed apple. I want to love him as I see him, I really do, but something is blocking me, preventing me. It scares me. Another voice in my head has been harping, wheedling, prevaricating.

"The guy's got his own private collection of World War II fighter airplanes that must be worth millions. It's totally fucking insane."

"That is totally fucking insane," one of the women says.

"All in mint condition, I might add."

"Damn."

"Trust fund baby?"

"You can be damn sure I'm investigating."

More champagne comes around on trays. And grilled shrimp on skewers. And small pastries stuffed with spicy ground pork. I decline. I've had enough. Mary stands next to Ed with her arms crossed. She looks ready to bolt. Zoo takes my hand in his. Sunday Smith looks my way and smiles. Is it a harmless, friendly smile? The look in her eye says she can see right through me, and she knows I'm only playing a part. Or am I just being paranoid?

11

When we return home Zoo takes me in his arms near the kitchen sink where we are filling our glasses of water to take to bed. He tells me I looked beautiful at the party.

"Really?"

"Yes, really."

He kisses me as if I'm some kind of food he's forgotten the taste of.

"Damiana Silver is going to invite us to dinner."

"Seriously? She said that to you?"

"Yes." I can see the excitement in Zoo's eyes. I'm sorry now that I brought it up. It has ruined the one romantic moment we've had in a long time.

"Tell me exactly what she said."

So I repeat what I remember of the conversation. Zoo pumps his fist in the air. "Yes!"

He undresses me in the bedroom until I am wearing my brown suit head to toe. His adrenaline is pumped. His desire for me stirs my own, and I take his suit of white into me. I want to give him pleasure, and I want him to think of mine. I grasp his shoulders, and he crouches over me like a predatory animal that wants to eat me alive. With his quick hard thrusts I can feel the hunger in him. But I don't want his hunger tonight. I want tenderness and the slow melt of time. I want what I had with the *other*.

I run my hands down his back, over the mounds of his buttocks. His body is tense. What I want more than anything is not to think. To just feel. To let my body make the calls. My hips jut upward, my neck arches back, my tongue swallows his. He seems to like this. His pitch increases, and he push-ups against the bed, his hands bookending my shoulders, and his hair flies loose and easy, and from my bottom view I peek my eyes open to see his eyelids laminated shut. His face is flush with the oncoming flood, and our bodies sink together into the depths of the mattress.

Zoo is by my side, asleep now, making peaceful animal sounds that shift with each breath. The clock glows midnight. I could work on my dissertation. I should work on the chapter on Akka. She rejected one life to find another, wandered naked and exposed, driven by a singular vision of Shiva. The eternal lover. Erotic and ascetic. Half this, half that. More and more I have a glimmer into the workings of her soul.

I break through my inertia, wrap up in my robe, steal out of bed, replace the covers gently around the deeply sleeping giant, put water on for tea, and dig Akka's poems from my backpack. By the small light of the kitchen, I read.

Better than joy
Of parting after having met
Is, O my dear, the joy
Of meeting after parting for a while.
I cannot for a moment live apart
When he is out of sight.
When shall I taste the joy
Of parting from my lord white as jasmine
Yet never more to part?

I'm puzzled. How can there be joy in parting? I look again at her words. Parting can have so many meanings. It can be the physical act of leaving, or the metaphysical, I suppose. Still, either way, wouldn't there be pain in that for her? Where does the joy come from? I feel rising panic. The deadline. This should be so easy. *Help, help.*

Then, no sooner do I wish it, and he comes. He enters the room tiptoeing. His eyes dart around like a thief. Like he is up to no good, and he knows it. I watch him carefully. He comes closer. I see the dark blue stain on his neck, like a patch of spilled ink; the stain from swallowing the poison that saved the world. I want so badly to touch it.

He takes my hand. His skin is luxuriously soft and moist, as if he has been birthed just then. He pulls me from the desk. He throws his tiger skin on the floor and lays himself down. Every naked muscle gleams with strength. He pulls me on top of him. The heavy perfume of all the flower garlands is intoxicating. I can hardly resist. I touch the stain. I wonder if I were to prick it with my fingernail, would the poison spurt out, and would that then end existence?

He licks me, and it feels like a flame is rising up my neck and across my cheek. His cobra snakes up my leg. I am upside down with desire, and I want to devour him. My breasts are screaming if my tongue is not.

He enters me, and I feel the blue heat spread in gentle waves up through my loins.

Through the layers of my belly and over my breasts.

I expose myself to ecstasy, and when it comes I am in a great wilderness.

Beasts have been set free. My own voice is musical. And a great many languages are being spoken at once. A songbird outpouring, multi-throated. The taste is sweet and spicy; the light is insanely blue and lovely. It sparkles like the ocean under the sun and bounces off his body, and I don't know where it comes from; it's just there like a warm bath of light.

As our bodies separate, I feel incredible joy. I can't believe it. I can't believe this. I stare into his face and what looks back at me are eyes that are soft and welcoming and joyful, like I've arrived in some place I've always meant to be.

And then he is gone.

No, no, I say as, in my dream, I float away on a boat down a river and all around me is the wild chatter of monkeys and parrots and the far away sound of an ambulance siren.

My eyes flutter open. I'm on the sofa. Did I dose off? How did I get here? I look around. My papers are as I left them on the kitchen table. I must have walked over to the sofa to lie down. At the kitchen table I stare down at the page, at the poem I've been working on. And then I see it. She is referring to the moment of separating after making love. The joy of *that*. Didn't I just feel that? It rises in me again, like a balloon.

I retranslate.

>*Better than the ecstasy of our bodies pulling apart,*
>*my dear,*
>*is the thrill of meeting after an absence*
>
>*I cannot for a moment live apart*
>*When you are out of my sight*
>*I cannot live*
>
>*How shall I taste the rapture again*
>*Of reuniting*
>
>*Lord, white as jasmine*
>*Without ever being apart?*

I peck away on my computer, and compose in academic language, but with the dream alive in me. Akka gives me plenty of evidence to argue the case for transcendence by the mystic poet. She has made Shiva a lover, as real as any flesh and blood one, and by doing so she has obliterated boundaries between human and god. I can argue how these complicated feelings of sexual and metaphysical love cannot be held within the confines of orthodox religion. How syntactically speaking, the word "parting" can contain multiple layers of meaning. Even Vanderoe might approve of that.

It is one-thirty before I tuck myself back into bed, worn and exhausted. Mystified. What just happened? Zoo's arms are flung apart, his legs straddle either end of the bed, having taken advantage of my absence. I gently shove him over. I'm ashamed for my own paltry passion. For the love poetry I can't write for Zoo.

12

Zoo shakes me awake.

"Wake up!" he says urgently.

"Why?" I ask, my voice thick, my mind even thicker.
"It's eight o'clock!"

But how can it be evening? My lips are singed and dry, my eyes pasted shut. Of course it's not night. It's morning, and daylight invades in a nasty way when I take my first blink.

"What were you dreaming about?" Zoo asks. "You were chattering away at four in the morning."

I stare into his face as if I am in the depths of a lake under a wall of ice. The dream that started on the sofa must have come back in the middle of the night.

"Gibberish," Zoo says. "A lot of moaning and groaning, too." He stares down at me.

It's a good thing my brown skin hides the guilty blush that rises into my face. I will have to hide my dream deep in the grave of my throat, bury *him* there. My secret pudding.

Zoo sits back down at his computer screen and is bathed in its cool glow.

"Maybe it was those shrimp skewers at the party," I say. It seems a plausible excuse.

"Didn't touch the food myself," Zoo says.

Of course not, I think. Zoo shuts down his computer. He is already dressed and showered and ready to go. He stuffs papers into his briefcase. He whistles. "Dinner with Richard Silver. Close the deal," Zoo says with a big grin on his face.

"When will you be home?" I ask, dutifully.

"Early. To have dinner with my gorgeous wife."

Words that would have been music to my ears yesterday. Now I feel guilt for the happiness I don't feel.

Zoo comes over and prods my body. "Going to lounge about all day?"

I turn my back to him and wait to hear the door click shut. I walk over to the windows that front the street. I watch the movement of cars and people down below. My eyes fix on a girl in a navy-blue blazer and pleated khaki skirt that she must have rolled up because it is much shorter than her school could possibly allow. Her legs stretch long and lanky. She unloads her schoolgirl's backpack from her shoulders and pulls a pack of cigarettes from the front. She lights the cigarette with a kind of professional ease. Apparently she is in no hurry to arrive at her destination. She is Akka's age, thirteen going on sixteen going on? A golden leaf falls from the tree she is leaning against and gently grazes her head. She picks it up from where it has fallen near her penny loafers and turns it over in her hand. She reaches into her backpack again and pulls out a heavy textbook that she balances on her knee. She lays the leaf gently between its pages, the cigarette dangling from her lips. She is so dreamy and young, caught between her fresh-born and has-been self. I feel myself caught in the same intersection, so alive in the dream, so weighed down when I wake up.

I remind myself I must get dressed and get to the conference. There will be a whole day of talks. I turn to the closet and sift through my clothes. I would like to wear something that would please *him*. A way to say thank you for his help last night. I find a blue silk salwar kameez. I spray perfume on myself and put gold earrings in my ears and line my eyes with black *kajal*. Looking at myself in the mirror, I find myself smiling brightly. It's okay, I think. It's a game.

13

ey, girl," Jangles calls out, and I must have been deep in my daze because I am surprised by her voice booming out to me. I stop my brisk walk and make my way to her.

"You're looking fine," she says, taking me in.

I thank her.

"I need to show you something," she says and pulls out a photo from inside her coat, and I can see she is thick with layers. It's a picture of a cow. She holds out a glossy, if worn and creased, 8x10 photo of a cow. It's actually two photos, a close-up of the cow's head on the top of the page and a wider shot of the cow standing in a pasture with some other cows in the background, and in the far distance a barn. It is a nice looking cow, white with classic black patches, and it looks well fed.

"That's my cow," she says. "Name's Tonya. I adopted her." In the close-up Tonya exhibits classic cow looks. Eyes with down-turned gaze, the slight cock of the head, furry ears forever pointed up, nostrils a baby's hand could fit in. On closer look, she appears to have a cleft lip.

"Yeah," she says. "You can adopt a cow, and then they won't slaughter it. They treat it good, feed it good." She stares into her picture, into the big, somnambulant eyes of Tonya. As if she is staring into the eyes of her own daughter.

This woman has so little, and here she is saving cows.

"You can adopt a cow, too. You get to name it; they send you pictures of it. I have all the information. You wanna see it?"

"What got you started on this?" I ask her.

"I've got to do some good in the world," she says, pulling a crumpled piece of paper from her pocket, an ad for the organization that promotes the adoption.

I look at the ad, but start to feel anxious about the conference and all the work waiting for me. Duck's translations and the new chapters that were supposed to be on Vanderoe's desk yesterday. The first talk will be starting in fifteen minutes. A warm autumn breeze gusts from nowhere and lifts my dress. I hastily push it down. A hot tingle travels up my spine. I feel a presence behind me. Has someone walked up? I turn to look.

A man stands next to me. I gasp. The man with the baseball cap. But he acts as if he doesn't know me. He picks up a used watch and examines it.

"Eh, mister, would you like to adopt a cow?" Jangles thrusts the picture of her cow in front of the man.

He looks at the pictures. "I like cows," he says and hands the picture back to Jangles.

"Have we met before?" I ask the man, hoping he will look at me, recognize me. "You look familiar."

His gaze is serene and steady. His skin smooth.

"*Namaste*," he says, folding his hands in prayer. But he does not acknowledge me beyond that.

I return the greeting.

"You are a good woman," he says to Jangles and walks off.

I want to chase after him, but Jangles takes my hand, and the bracelets rattle just under her coat sleeve. "Only cost ten dollars a month," she says. "Can you spare that?"

"No, I don't think so. Not right now." I keep my eyes on the man as he moves further down the block.

"You don't want to, you don't want to. Nothing I can do about it."

"I'm sorry, so sorry," I say, rushing away. "Maybe next time."

"Scarf look good on you!" She calls out when I've moved three steps away. I turn, and we look at each other. I smile haplessly. The turquoise scarf is wrapped around my neck. When I turn back around, he's gone.

14

I'm still shaken up when I reach my office. I hear Duck's heavy, off-beat footsteps approaching my door. My heart races. I collect myself. Duck has someone who she wants to introduce to me. He is here for the conference, a scholar visiting from Santa Barbara, Dr. Veeraswamy. He greets me with the traditional *namaste*, with his hands clasped in prayer, and I respond in kind. He dresses in traditional clothes, a crisply ironed white cotton *dhoti*, and looks appropriately distinguished with graying hair and horn-rimmed glasses that magnify his eyes.

"Walk with us to his talk," Duck says, and I gratefully exit my office and shut the door behind me.

"What is it you are studying?" Veeraswamy inquires as we walk side by side. I tell him the subject of my thesis. Poets, mystics, rebels, Shiva worshippers. *The little girl who talks to god.*

"Yes, yes," he says. "Then you will find my talk very interesting. Rig Veda, you know, has many prayers to Shiva."

I smile. "I've been looking forward to it," I say.

Duck reminds me that she has arranged a dinner at her

home in the evening. I promise her I will arrive early to help. There is a decent crowd for Dr. Veeraswamy considering it's the first seminar of the day. I take a seat next to Louis Gray, a fellow Ph.D. candidate who is slumping in his seat. He tells me he is on the verge of quitting. His wife is pregnant; he's got to get a job; he's thinking of teaching high school. He looks pale and shabby in clothes that are almost mock professorial, khaki pants and a navy blazer.

"But if you quit," I ask him, "where does that leave me?"

"Free," he says, "to hold up the flame." His smile is more like a grimace.

As Duck begins her introduction of Veeraswamy, Louis nudges me and nods towards the door. A man walks in. A stranger. My stomach tightens.

"Who's that?" Louis whispers.

I shake my head, but inside I'm in shock. I stiffen in my seat. The man is dressed much as Louis is, in khakis and a button-down shirt. But his long, black hair hangs loose well past his shoulders. All eyes shift momentarily to him. The energy shifts subtly in the room, as if super-charged electrons whirl around him. Louis is in the aisle seat, and I'm just next to him. The man comes to our row and squeezes past Louis and then me and sits in the empty seat next to mine. Louis sits to attention. I stare studiously forward, but I feel faint from the smell of jasmine.

Veeraswamy starts his talk by reading a verse from the Rig Veda. It is a passage poetically describing Shiva, invoking his power and his strength. *Let thy fury be restrained, do us no hurt!* I wish I could turn and see the expression on the man's face, but I keep my gaze stonily averted. Veeraswamy's voice is heavily incantatory and imbues the verse with inspirational meaning.

I feel his warm breath. It's all I can do not to turn and look at him. Every pore in my body is wide open.

"You see in the ancient days man turned to Shiva for protection from the fierce hand of Mother Nature. Or he turned to him for mercy. Spare *me*, he prayed. But what is the modern human being doing with this god? He is equally popular today as he has always been. It is the very complexity of his nature that has allowed him to survive. And it is matched by the complexity of modern life. We must hold so many realities at the same time. And which living person today does not desire some form of transformation?"

Louis nudges my elbow. He has me look over to Professor Casing, who has been around forever and who is sitting three rows down and to the side. His head is bowed down, gone a bit slack, dozing. Louis smiles.

"You see?" he whispers. "This is why we need to get out. Now."

But I am more awake than ever. I drink in Veeraswamy's every word. I want, I need, to know about this divine interloper. It's as if Veeraswamy has been sent especially for me.

"If we are born a cobbler's son, let us say for the sake of example, do we not wish to be a Bollywood movie star? If we are born ugly, we want to become beautiful. If poor, wealthy. If wealthy, then powerful. If unloved, loved. Shiva, too, holds complex realities in his very being. He is lust incarnate one moment, and meditating for a thousand years in the next. He is the very essence of passion: angry, fearful, vengeful, and yet he is purely sublime, peaceful, and serene. If anyone can bring about transformation, it is Shiva."

I dare to turn to look. The man has his eyes closed, his hands on his lap. He is barely breathing. Deep in meditation? I fight the pull towards him. To take his hand and caress my face with it. To hook my leg into his. Everything about my life before he showed up feels dead, dying, like I was a fallow field, waiting to be planted.

"You see with Shiva, all possibilities exist. Here in the West, you do not like contradiction. You enjoy rational, linear thought. Your heaven is up, your hell is down; you sit squarely in the middle terrified of life and death. We in the East have our stories, our myths, and our gods to provide us with the metaphysical wherewithal to exist in all three planes at once. We can survive change, the one constant, and death, well what is death, but mere *transformation*?"

Veeraswamy brings his lecture to a close. There is polite applause to which I add my own enthusiasm. Louis heads quickly for the door. I want to linger and speak with Veeraswamy, but Duck has him by the arm and is leading him away. I will corner him at the dinner tonight. I'm burning up with questions. The man remains seated next to me, meditating. Curious glances are thrown his way. I feel protective of him, contemptuous of those who don't understand. I want to shout, here is the real thing, right here in front of us. Wake up, people! And then I get a whiff of rot, of the nauseating odor of an unbathed body, of days of accumulated sweat and unlaundered clothes. I look more carefully. His hair is matted in dreadlocks. He turns and smiles at me. His mouth is full of rotted teeth. He's just some person who walked off the street. They show up at the university all the time. Perpetual students. Homeless people looking for dry heat. I hurry out of the lecture hall, breathing hard, my heart beating in a panic. What is happening to me? I rush to the next seminar. Stay the course. Stay the course. Eat my salad. Don't look over my shoulder, whatever I do.

15

Duck's home is a spacious and comfortable brownstone overstuffed with artifacts from her travels abroad. Brass lamps, Afghani tribal headgear, carved teak side tables, hand-embroidered Kashmiri throw pillows, temple miniatures from South India. The total effect robs the eyes of a resting place, but then Duck is like that, too, in constant motion. Duck's husband, George Dickey, is also a professor. Dr. & Dr. Dickey. He teaches European History. George is kindly and avuncular, and also witty and sharp. Between them, they are experts on almost half the world.

Zoo tried to beg out of this dinner, but, quid pro quo, I tell him I attended his business party, and he must attend mine. I reminded him he had promised to come home early to have dinner with me anyway. He was pissy all the way here, grumbling that he left a carcass of work on his desk, that he had nothing to say to academics, that his presence wouldn't make a difference.

"You don't belong in my world, and I don't belong in yours. Is that what you're saying?" I put it bluntly.

He sighed. "Christ almighty."

I help Duck with some last-minute preparations in the kitchen, and she appoints me official greeter while she makes a quick change into one of her gorgeous Indian outfits. Zoo settles in the living room with a glass of wine and George. Dr. Veeraswamy arrives exactly as one of Duck's clocks chimes seven times.

"Hallo, Hallo," he says enthusiastically, surveying me, surveying the room. I'm struck by his handsomeness. His salt-and-pepper hair cut short stands almost straight up on his head. He's slim and elegant with a black wool scarf around his neck and black glasses in a square frame, an old-fashioned style that has become hip and modern. George offers him a glass of wine, and he giggles and says he never takes alcohol. He requests juice. I tell him I loved his talk and apologize that he did not receive a larger audience. He tells me he is pleased, very pleased, to find some young Indians (me) taking interest in their cultural ancestry. In India, he tells me, the young people are only interested in Hollywood and Bollywood. I serve him juice, and just before I can pin him down with some questions, Vanderoe arrives with his wife. I tighten up, expecting a scolding, a grilling, an imperious stare, but Vanderoe spots Zoo in the living room and is much more interested in talking financial markets than my failings. He leaves me in peace with Veeraswamy.

Veeraswamy projects a kind warmth, something of the gentleman scholar. I feel I can ask him anything, and I will not be ridiculed. I've never had that privilege with Vanderoe, always tiptoeing around his brilliance and his contempt. We seat ourselves in a corner of Duck's living room.

"Are there any modern-day stories or reports of Shiva appearing in real life? I'm thinking of a modern day Akka Mahadevi."

Veeraswamy ponders. He says there are many who claim to be avatars, the obvious example being Satya Sai Baba. "In India," he says, "we have this continuous thread between past and present, so these things don't seem so strange. Anyone can claim to be the living incarnation of a god, and generally we don't question. It is the great strength and the great weakness of our tradition."

I feel drawn into his warmth, his natural intellectual curiosity. I risk telling him about my experience with Jangles on the street. How I prayed to Shiva, then this strange man showed up.

Veeraswamy's eyes widen. He likes the story. "You know it is fascinating," he says, "how we always speak of the knowledge we have gained as human beings. But we rarely speak of the knowledge we have lost. We have convenient amnesia for the past. That is why we need to keep looking at our ancient texts. But think how inadequate even those are. Before the written words there was a whole body of knowledge we have no access to. Maybe the kind of experience you describe was a routine experience at one time. How are we to know?"

I feel flush with gratitude that he has not dismissed what has happened as lunatic. Vanderoe walks up to us just as Veeraswamy is asking me when I will finish my Ph.D. "I'll be defending in May," I say. Vanderoe raises his eyebrows.

"Don't steal her away from us," he says.

Veeraswamy laughs. "Actually that is just what I was plotting. Our department is thin in Sanskrit scholarship. We could use some backup."

"A trade for a Byzantine would be useful, but Ellen would never allow it. This is her protégé, and you'd have to yank pretty hard to get her away."

My head ping-pongs back and forth between them, happy I am so wanted.

"Contingent on her finishing, of course. It's been what, ten, fifteen years?"

I laugh uneasily and look at Veeraswamy. He seems to know it's a joke. It's mean of Vanderoe to bring it up.

"Better late than never," I say, but my jaunty tone doesn't mask the nervousness I feel.

Duck calls us to the dinner table, and we have hardly passed the food around when Dr. Veeraswamy asks us very pointedly how we all manage to live in a country that is only concerned with one thing and only one thing.

"Oh, you must mean sports," George jokes.

"Money," Duck says, echoing my thoughts. But Veeraswamy shakes his head.

"No, no, not money. That concern is the world over."

I see Zoo nod in agreement across the table.

Vanderoe says America is obsessed with itself and its own nationalistic fervor.

"Sex," says Anna, Vanderoe's wife and former student, a Swedish beauty with translucent skin and evangelical blue eyes. She abandoned scholarship and started a small business selling handmade toys from felted wool.

Veeraswamy's face lights up.

"Yes! You are surrounded by it everywhere. You have exported this obsession overseas and to all corners of the world."

"What's wrong with sex?" Vanderoe asks with a mischievous smile on his face.

"What about the sacred sexual texts of India like the Kama Sutra and the Ananda Ranga?" I tease.

"What about the famous temple carvings of Konarak and Khujaraho where hundreds of sexual positions are carved in stone in graphic detail? What about all the stories of the gods cavorting about? America did not invent advertising sex," Duck adds.

Veeraswamy smiles.

"The difference, I believe, is that in ancient India you will find that sex, or the physical, if you will, is always in balance with the spiritual and the intellectual. But in the modern world that we are living in, the physical and the material have taken over all. Where is the spiritual? It has become a commodity, a big business. And the intellectual? Who even reads a book anymore?"

"This is not a modern conflict at all," Vanderoe says. "Think Greece. Think fertility gods and goddesses, Apollo, Dionysus, Eros. The hedonist and the Spartan. Man has always been at war with himself."

"The idea of balance is simply an ideal," Duck says. "Once humans were cast out of the garden we were forever condemned to be out of balance. And we shall forever seek it."

Zoo says that unlike the ancient world, humans now expect their physical and material needs to be met. "Go tell someone who is starving that they should find balance in their lives. What a joke," he says.

"Your point of view is the one that dominates the world today," Veeraswamy says pointedly to Zoo, almost scolding him. "But it is becoming more and more clear that the earth cannot support our human appetites. Man without god," Veeraswamy continues, "is a danger to the planet. Without reverence, awe, and fear we will continue our relentless rape of the earth. However, man with god is a danger to humanity, always killing and destroying in the name of religion. So how do we find the middle ground?"

For a moment the table is quiet, our minds bent to the gravity of Veeraswamy's voice, the sincerity and depth of his inquiry. Veeraswamy has given me the idea to find the middle ground. A patch I can safely stand on. Where the waters that seem to be rising won't be able to touch me.

16

I unload groceries onto the kitchen counter, squash and leeks for soup, and salad greens, a small seeded baguette, and milk and eggs, and listen to the public radio version of the day's news. A feel-good piece about a woman scientist whose theories were dismissed and ridiculed and then proven to be true. Probably her nemesis was someone like Vanderoe. I have spent two days counting the number of times Akka uses nature as a metaphor for her feelings. The more birds and trees and flowers and fruit I count the further I feel I am getting from the finishing line. It's like putting money in a bank you know is on the verge of insolvency. My body is restless. My toes itch with desire. *He.* Who is *he?* That's what I want to know. I've combed her poems for the answer. She is all about the search. *This world haunts me, what should I do, O lord what should I do about this constant turmoil within me?*

The conversation with Dr. Veeraswamy inspired me to dig in. If transformation is the key, then being open to it is a necessity. Allowing the door to be unlocked.

It's in the cheerful musical interlude between news stories that Zoo returns from work. He's got a package the size of a Roman bust in his arms. He struggles through the door, and I run over and help relieve him of his briefcase and computer bag.

"What's this?"

"A surprise."

There's so much brown paper clothed around the package, and bubble wrap swathed under that, not to mention the yards of tape, that it takes a lot of concentrated ripping and cutting to work our way through to the result.

A lamp. Zoo steps back with a great deal of satisfaction and pride. I don't know what I expected, an amazing, blinking, whirring, whizzing popping machine?

"Don't you love it?" Zoo says. He shakes off the remaining bits of clinging paper and sets it on the side table by the sofa. He leans down and plugs the lamp into the socket. A simple push on the floor button, and it comes to life.

"We needed light in that corner," Zoo says. He slings his arm over my shoulder, and we stand facing the lamp, admiring the latest addition to our home furnishings.

I try and muster up some excitement for Zoo's purchase, for the perfect glow of diffused light through the white glass shade shaped like a mushroom, and the polished chrome of the stand and base, but instead I feel consumed with an unfamiliar anger.

"Don't you like it?"

"It's okay."

"That's all? Okay? It's Italian milk glass."

"It fits," I say.

Zoo takes a look at me. "You're angry because you didn't choose it with me."

"No, not at all."

"Yes, that's it."

I turn away quickly and walk to the kitchen. I get busy washing and chopping the vegetables. I push thoughts of *him* down. How could he be more real than what is in front of me?

Zoo pulls a frosty Lite beer from the fridge. He's worried that we haven't gotten a call for dinner with the Silvers.

"Maybe Damiana was just playing with us," he says.

"Maybe," I say.

"What's gotten into you? Do you not care about anything anymore?"

I turn to him, startled. "Of course I do," I say, guilty. I leave the soup to its simmering. I pull Zoo over to the sofa and like any good wife would do, I massage the back of his neck. He softens under my touch. Little moans escape from his mouth. I work my strong hands deeply into his flesh into the space between his shoulder blades where the tension of his day is lodged.

"It's a beautiful lamp, don't you think?"

"How much was it?" I ask.

"We'll be fine."

"That much?"

"Yeah."

"Why?"

"Just wanted it."

"My turn," I say, shifting around so my feet are in his lap. He digs into the soles with his thumb. Fierce pain erupts from the bottom of my foot, and I snap it away.

"Ouch! Too hard." He pulls the foot back into his lap and presses again, softer this time.

"Zoo, where does this end?"

"What?"

"The more we spend, the harder you have to work, the less we see each other—do we even know each other any more?"

"I haven't changed. Same old Niles. You're the one."

"I just want—"

"Dinner ready?"

I think of Veeraswamy. I say it. "Transformation."

Zoo presses into my foot again. Then drops it to the floor. "You're too tight. Loosen up. Start your transformation there."

"I've seen him again."

"Who?"

"Shiva."

Zoo looks at me. I tell him about Jangles and the cows.

"So he showed up to tell you to adopt cows?"

"I didn't," I say, "I didn't do it."

Soup and salad and French bread are mostly a silent affair. No matter how hard I try, I can't muster enthusiasm for a lamp. Or a promotion.

"Soup's a bit creamy," Zoo mumbles.

"Sorry," I say.

The salad is like cud in my mouth. If only I had four stomachs with which to digest it.

17

Rebecca Leigh's office is being cleared out. I see an older man and a younger man hauling boxes out of it. I go over and introduce myself. The older man is her father, the younger her brother. They tell me she is back in her home and has instructed them to get everything out of the office. I want to tell them to stop, she's making a mistake, but they are hurried and anxious to get the job done.

The last time I spoke with her she sounded shaky. I could hear the bleakness in her voice. I go back to my office and call her.

"I'm done, Anjali," she says. "My life isn't worth a piece of paper."

We agree that I should come out to Brooklyn, where she lives. She says she doesn't want to step foot in Manhattan, and certainly not within shouting distance of the university.

I take the train out to Brooklyn late one afternoon. A stiff wind is pulling leaves off trees and the sky threatens rain as I walk the seven blocks from the train station to her apartment. I feel nervous, I don't know what to say. I've never known anyone before who has tried to end his or her life. I bought some cookies and brownies and lemon bars, and they are in a pretty pink box wrapped in a yellow ribbon. I hope the sweets will help ease the way.

She opens the door in her pajamas. Her long, brown hair is pulled back in a messy ponytail. We hug, and I'm pleasantly surprised by the warmth of her body and the little bit of extra flesh I can fold myself around. She murmurs thanks for the sweets and says the meds have made her fat, but she doesn't care. She puts the kettle on for tea, and we sit on her sofa that's strewn with catalogs with pictures of horses and riders. I don't see any evidence of her books around. The boxes must have gone into storage.

"I know it was stupid," she says. "But it's in the past now. I'm not going to dwell on it. I'm moving on."

"What will you do?" I ask her.

"I don't know. Go out West maybe." She flips through one of the magazines and hands me a page to look at—pictures of people riding on wide-open meadows with purple mountains in the background.

"How are you? Are you okay?" she asks with genuine concern.

"Yes. I'm fine," I say.

"You don't look fine," she says. "You look thin."

I laugh. "Zoo says we're getting fat."

"Men," she says. "I thought I was fine, too, but I wasn't. Obviously." She scowls. "I will never, ever let a man dictate to me how I should feel about myself. Ever."

"Do you mean Van—"

"Yes, him." She interrupts me before I can finish saying his name.

The kettle whistles, and Rebecca gets up to make the tea. I follow her into her kitchen and watch her pour hot water into a teapot filled with leaves.

"Do you want to know the worst thing? He hasn't called. Once. Prick. You should quit, Anjali. Please. I don't want to see what happened to me happen to you. The man is a pig."

I don't know what to say to her. I have no love for Vanderoe. But I don't want to be defeated by him. I don't want to belittle her decision either. I can't tell her I have felt protected by Shiva. I've felt safe. That I've had divine intervention, and he is stronger than Vanderoe. I don't want to freak her out with some religious conversion. It isn't what it is.

Rebecca looks out the window, out to some distant place. I look out there, too. All I can see is the mangle of telephone wires against a quickly darkening sky.

18

A desperate call comes from my mother. Nita has an unexpected pregnancy. She has decided to have an abortion, and she wants to have it in Chicago.

"You come," my mother implores. "We don't know what to do with this girl."

The last thing I want to do is go home. I will have to mediate Nita's latest drama, protect her from my parents' anger, salve their shame, their hurt. I can already imagine the pained look on their faces; the hope for grandchildren has become central to their conversation. They have been pressuring me. Zoo's anxious that Damiana's going to call while I'm gone, and we will have to miss the dinner.

I fly into O'Hare, and Papa is waiting at the airport. He looks morose, and beard stubble covers his face in rough patches. He wears his heavy winter coat and woolen cap and scarf. When I hug him I feel like I am hugging a bear in hibernation. We have to wait in the terminal for Nita's flight; she's arriving an hour and a half after me. We sit at a mirrored bar, and Papa orders two beers. The hanging television is tuned to CNN, and there is news of a freshly declared heightened state of alert for the Thanksgiving holiday next week.

I ask Papa not to be angry with Nita. He looks at me for a moment.

"She is irresponsible," he says coldly.

"Mistakes can happen," I say, the familiar role of eldest and supposedly wisest wearing thin on me.

He sips his beer. "Don't worry about me," he says. "Your mother has instructed me to keep my mouth shut."

"So how are you anyway?" I ask.

"They are talking of buying out our company."

"Who?"

"Some bigger company."

"Are you worried?" Papa looks at me as if I have just asked the dumbest question on earth.

"Of course I am worried. But it is out my hands. So I must just go along."

"Maybe you should look for another job."

"I have been working twenty-five years for these people. Who will hire me? I might lose my retirement, my benefits, everything I have worked for. They can just get rid of me if they like."

"They wouldn't do that. They can't."

My father scoffs. "I should have changed jobs long ago. I could have made much more money. Only now I am realizing in this country you do not give your loyalty to one company. My brother has received retirement housing in Bangalore, a good pension, even a gold watch. I will be lucky to get a ball-point pen."

I feel sad for my father, and sadder still for the son I know he wishes he had. The son who would bring him security in his old age, no matter what happened. A son who would provide, out of filial duty and obligation, a final resting home for my parents. Daughters are given away to the husband's family and can't be relied on for anything, although I have always maintained that I can do anything a son can.

When Nita arrives, her plane a half hour late, she brings an energetic hostility with her. It's apparent in her outfit, low cut jeans and a ripped cotton sweatshirt that hovers just above her belly button and impossibly tall high heels, apparel sure to rankle our parents. I wish she understood that a little contrition would go a long way. I look for signs of pregnancy, a fuller face, a thicker frame, but find none. She is as lithe and pretty as ever, her black hair cut to stylish and bouncy shoulder length, her face made up subtly with eyeliner and lipstick, nothing overdone.

She hugs and kisses me, and gives Papa a stiff peck. He wastes no time with greetings, turns quickly and leads us out of the airport. On the way home, Nita spreads herself in the back seat of the car and talks on her cell phone, chattering away about things I can't understand with people I don't know. I know she has a wide circle of friends in Atlanta, but I have no clue who the father of this baby might be. When we finally pull into the driveway of our home, a split-level colonial with green window shutters and white aluminum siding that virtually glows in the dark, I feel both elated that I don't live here anymore and sad that so much of my childhood took place here. The lawn is more brown than green, and the yews have their tops barbered off.

Mama waits at the door. She's three inches shorter than me, so I can wrap her up in my arms and kiss the top of her head. Nita towers over her even more than I do.

"What smells so good?" I ask.

"You girls must be hungry."

"I'm starved," Nita says.

Mama heats up the food in the microwave, and she, Nita, and I sit at the kitchen table eating *chapattis* and spiced cauliflower and potato *sabzii*. Papa takes his food in the living room and switches from the shopping channel to the late news. The volume is irritatingly loud, and I hear the same cycle of news repeated that we heard in the bar.

"So who is the father?" I ask Nita.

She rolls her eyes. "Nobody."

I can see how this answer hurts my mother. The idea of having sex with 'nobody' and getting pregnant must make every bone in her body ache in protest.

"Does he know?" I ask Nita.

She nods. "He's married, okay. He has a family and everything. I met him at a job-training seminar. He was leading the whole damn thing. Good enough? Don't ask me any more questions."

Mama starts crying softly, putting her head in her hands. I put an arm around her shoulder.

"Mom, it's no big deal, really," Nita says.

"It is to her and Papa," I say.

"It was a stupid mistake. I'm going to be more careful

next time."

Mama continues to wipe away tears.

"I should have just taken care of this in Atlanta," Nita says. "It was a mistake to come home."

"Who is going to take care of you if not your family?" my mother asks.

Nita walks over to the cupboard and roots out a box of crackers. She slumps back at the table eating directly out of the carton. Her crunching sounds carnivorous. Mama wipes her tears on the back of her hand. Papa comes into the kitchen and sets his plate by the sink. He fills a glass of water. He still has his knit cap on.

"Will you make my Ovaltine?" he asks Mama.

She nods.

"Can I have Ovaltine?" Nita asks.

I chime in that I want some, too.

Mama heats up some milk and pretty soon we settle into the living room with our steaming cups of hot Ovaltine. I turn the television off. The furniture is a pastiche of styles, mostly department store offerings of plaids and florals, unwieldy glass-topped tables and faux-wood bureaus. I feel safe here amongst the familiar surroundings. The smells of Indian cooking have permeated the walls.

"Remember when we first came to America?" I ask. "And we lived in that apartment above the shoe store? And we found that stained-glass contact paper, and we stuck it on all those windows in the living room. And there were all the air bubbles, and we couldn't get them out?"

Nita laughs. Even Papa smiles.

"Those were good days," Mama says.

"Where did we go wrong?" Papa says.

"When I was thirteen and you made me act in the Diwali play about Rama and Sita," Nita says. "I hated that."

Papa looks puzzled. "No one made you do that."

Nita laughs a short vicious laugh.

"This is the first time we've all been together in a long time," I say, trying again to bring us together in an affectionate way.

"Well, you can thank me for that," Nita says.

"When will you start to take your life seriously?" Papa says, directing the dam-has-burst flood of anger right at her.

"Keep quiet," Mama says. "Let's just enjoy this time together."

"I do take my life seriously," Nita replies. "I just happened to get pregnant."

"But you are twenty-nine, and you have not found a suitable husband. You go making yourself available to every Tom, Dick, and Harry who comes around."

"Is that what you think? That's sick. You are a sick human being."

Papa starts coughing, the deep asthmatic rumble shaking his body.

"Enough," Mama says, anxiously. "We are just lonely. We want you girls to be happy. We want you to have children, give us some grandchildren. That is all."

"It's sick to call your own daughter a slut."

"I don't think that is what he was saying, Nita. I think he's just worried about you," I say.

Nita looks over at me. "You have the goddamn grand-children," she screams, turning to face me full on. "What are you waiting for?"

She's out of her chair and in her bedroom, slamming the door behind her, leaving us in a decapitated silence.

19

The next morning, at the doctor's office, Nita fills out all the paperwork in a hurry. She is paying with cash, and handles everything with efficiency. The nurse informs me I must return to pick her up in two hours. I drive to our old neighborhood, Devon, the Little India of Chicago. I park the car and walk down the main street. There are dress shops with the latest glitzy fashions from India on display and jewelry shops and Indian grocery shops and many restaurants. The smell of curries and fried snacks makes me hungry. There is the medical office building where Papa set up his first radiology practice, before joining the company he is now afraid of being axed from. I walk past the apartment building we used to live in. The shoe store is now a cellular phone shop. Upstairs I see the fake stained glass windows are still there. Who would want the nasty job of removing all the hardened glue? Looking at the building, and remembering being a young girl there, I can't see the road from there to where I am now. Mama's and Papa's sad faces from last night haunt me. I'm sure they can't see the road either. Each step an attempt at a better life. From the dusty village to big city Bangalore. From Bangalore to Chicago. From city to the suburbs. From medical technician to chief radiologist. From village girl to shopping channel addict. When we immigrated from India we got the better life, but we stayed married to something older and deeper. Nita's the only one who fully embraced the change.

I see a flash of blue through the glass window of East West Imports. Is it just a reflection? I can't tell. The thick glass of the storefront window blurs my ability to see inside. As I enter, I set off the tinkle of a series of small bells. A petite woman sitting by the cash register acknowledges me. It is a warren of trinkets, jewelry, candles, prayer rugs, and religious icons from India, Nepal, and China. There is flute music playing through small speakers and incense burning. I feel a warm current of air. It draws me to the far corner of the shop, but there is no one there. I spot a Shiva lingam on the shelf. It fits perfectly in my palm, a polished black stone the shape and size of an elongated egg set in the traditional base of matching stone. The symbolic phallus in the vulva. I feel its smooth surface, its pleasing weight. He is embodied in a stone. Memories of my maternal grandparents' altar stir in me. They had a Shiva lingam and a Ganesh, the elephant god, and a brass statue of Rama and Sita. I can even hear my grandmother's singsong voice chanting prayers. My grandfather used to go to the garden to cut fresh flowers to place in the altar and then sit cross-legged in front of it with his hands folded in deep meditation. I find a little pocket brass Ganesh and a plaster-painted Saraswati and a brass *diwa* in which I will be able to put a tea light. I look around again, but I'm the only one in the shop.

I pause at a stack of colorful posters of the Indian gods. Leafing through the pantheon, Ganesh, Krishna, Lakshmi, Vishnu, I find a dancing blue Shiva. He is resplendent with the crescent moon tucked in his crown of hair, a giant cobra entwining his neck, his four arms carving the air, one holding a blazing fire, the other a drum beating the rhythm of the universe, his hair flying off his back, his tiger-skin loin cloth wrapped around his waist. I feel the pull to him. I want him, his energy, his danger, his succulence, his help.

I take my items to the counter, and the cashier rings them up. The shop owner takes a dust rag and wipes off the lingam at the counter. She wears her hair parted down the middle, and her long, black braid reminds me of all my aunts in India. Her eyes are lined with black eyeliner. Her face has a sweet, wrinkled grace to it.

I ask her which incense she is burning. The heavy pungent smell fills me with nostalgia for my grandparents.

She hands me a thin rectangular cardboard box. "You take it, she says. Gift from me." She places her hand over mine. "You light incense and pray for peace for my country. For Tibet."

"I will," I say. "Thank you." I pay my thirty-nine ninety-five and say goodbye. When I step out into the street I see a man at the corner. A baby-blue knit cap. *No.* He turns and walks down a side street. I follow. When I turn the corner, he has gained distance on me. His pace is brisk, and he never turns to look back.

20

I think of Akka wandering. Searching. Barefoot. Naked. Did she see him walking in front, always just steps away. I like walking. The forward movement of it. The obliteration of thought. Maybe this is what she felt. I feel that I'm both inside my body and outside of it. Watching myself following blindly. No fear. As if being drawn by a rope. Closer and closer.

I see him enter through the gate of a small park. When I reach the park myself, I see him sitting on a cement bench that faces a stone fountain, the water turned off for the winter. Leaves have collected over the pavement and in the small garden beds, the plants brown and dying. Something about him is different. Is it him? He has the bulk of a construction worker but the wool coat of an office employee. I sit on the bench across from him. The man smiles at me. Gives me a little hand wave. I wave back.

The man closes his eyes and leans his head back to soak up the winter sun. I can't tell. Have I just followed an ordinary man to a small city park? It's unnerving. I close my eyes too and lean my head back. A voice startles me. "Do you understand the nature of the unmanifest?" My eyes pop open. But the man has not moved. He is still leaning back, tanning himself. I close my eyes again. I absorb the quietness of the park. A crow caws somewhere nearby. Leaves rattle in a dry wind.

I see him as I saw him in my dream. Those loving eyes. Those rounded and strong shoulders. No, I don't understand the unmanifest. I don't comprehend much of anything. I don't know how you can live two lives at once. Akka ran away from the king. She left her parents. Stripped down to her hair. How did Akka do it? That's what I want to ask him.

He is sitting tall, with his head balanced perfectly on his shoulders and back. He brings the palms of his two hands together in front of his chest. Prayer position. His long, tapered fingers, with beautifully polished nails glimmer in the nameless room of my mind.

I lose myself in him. I feel as if he is breathing with me, each rise and fall of my breath matches his. Each breath tastes so delicious, like a morsel to be savored, turned over by the tongue, digested before the next bite and the next bite. Paying attention to each breath, time slows to a virtual stillness.

She devoted herself to me, he says in a quiet off-screen voice. *"Can you do that?"*

That will take time, I say.

I have time, he says. *I have an eternity.*

21

Nita yells at me. "Where the fuck are you?" I don't know how many times my cell phone has rung. When I finally answer, I am shocked. I was supposed to pick her up more than an hour ago. The man is gone from the park. I rush back through the streets, only guessing how I might have come, listening for the sounds of the main road. By the time I reach my car, I am out of breath. How did I let this happen?

Nita takes one look at me and swallows her anger. "Jesus, she says, what happened to you?"

I tell her I went to our old neighborhood and got lost.

If she weren't tired and out of it herself, she would have quizzed me more thoroughly. I feel as if I've committed a crime and managed to slip the police.

That night, Nita in her pajamas and uncombed hair, makes my mother happy by eating enough for a family of ten. I force myself to talk about anything that comes to my head; politics, a play Zoo and I went to, the global economic picture. If I talk and act normal, act as I have done all these years, I feel sure I can keep control of myself.

After dinner, I show my father the passage I am translating for Duck. He reads the Sanskrit out loud. His fluent and melodic reading is a pleasure to hear. It's captivating to watch his face, tired as it is, come to life with these words. After that, I have him read some of the poems of Akka Mahadevi in the original Kannada. But he doesn't have to look at the book. He knows many of them by heart. Some other father emerges from the reading and reciting. It's the father I never really appreciated when I was forced to sit for what seemed to be hours on end learning what seemed to be an impossibly dead language. Like Nita devouring dinner, he eats these words up.

He tells me that his grandmother had a particular affinity for Akka Mahadevi. That she spent many hours every day in *puja* to Shiva and that she neglected her own children and her husband.

"Our great-grandmother?" I ask, surprised.

He nods. "Her husband's family sent her back to her parents, she was in her forties then, but her own family didn't want her. In those days, no one wanted a grown daughter in their house. Just one more mouth to feed. They kicked her out, and she ended up being a servant in someone's household. Then she grew too old to work. She would have died on the street, but my father, your grandfather, took pity on her and let her in."

It shocks me that I never knew this story.

"Did you know her?" I ask.

Papa nods. "I was always finding her false teeth for her. She was very kind to me, saving me sweets from the temple. She would recite these poems of Akka Mahadevi day and night.

On fast days, she would go out in the street stark naked, and we would be sent running to bring her home. It was very humiliating for our family. My mother disliked her and treated her very badly. She would only give her the minimal amount of food, two chapattis and some vegetables. My grandmother would beg for a little rice and curds, but my mother would curse at her; you can't imagine the horrible things she would say, and then my father would scream at my mother for being so stingy."

I ask my father if he has a picture of my great-grandmother.

He has me bring over a photo album from the bookshelf. The pages are filled with old black-and-white photos, taken in a photo studio; everyone dressed in formal wear for the official recording of the family portrait. My father was only ten-years old, and amidst his five brothers and one sister, he looks like every other scrawny kid with big eyes and large protruding teeth. He points out my great-grandmother to me, a slight woman standing at the very edge of the family, short and bent over, her sari covering her head, her hands folded in prayer, her forehead marked with three horizontal stripes of ash, the characteristic emblem of Shiva worshippers. I understand even more clearly now why I must clearly illuminate the world of Akka in my Ph.D. She did not exist outside of history. This is what Vanderoe doesn't understand.

"You look like her," Nita says, looking over my shoulder. My father nods, agreeing with Nita. The resemblance is clear, the oval face, the long forehead and straight, short nose. If I lost a few more pounds until my ribs showed, I could easily stand in for her. A chill drives through me. I don't want to know this.

22

When I return home to Manhattan, mid-day, I relish the quiet of the empty apartment. It was hard to say goodbye to my parents. I felt the familiar rush of guilt and sadness. My mother cried. My father recited the same verse from the old play by Kalidasa, the story of Sakuntala when she leaves her father's house. *"My heart is touched with sadness since Sakuntala must go today, my throat is choked with sobs, my eyes are dulled by worry—if a disciplined ascetic suffers so deeply from love, how do fathers bear the pain of each daughter's parting?"* I couldn't help but tear up and so did he.

I unpack my clothes and tuck the bag with the lingam and other purchases deep into a drawer. I resolve to make a fresh start. I will catch up on my translations for Duck; I will keep my work scholarly and dispassionate; I will take care of myself; I will take care of Zoo; and I will call the plumbers to come fix the faulty air duct that blows cold air instead of hot, as he has asked me to do, I see, on the note left for me on the kitchen counter.

I check the messages and am surprised to hear one from Richard Silver's secretary. We are invited to dinner with Richard and Damiana in three weeks, and can I kindly RSVP at my earliest convenience.

I call Zoo right away and confirm that we have nothing planned for the first Friday in December, and he is absolutely thrilled; I can hear it in his voice, although he is playing it very cool and acting very busy and just barks at me to go ahead and RSVP in the affirmative.

"And by the way," he tells me, "we are having Thanksgiving with Ed and Mary."

When Zoo comes home, well after dinnertime, he's whistling.

"I hear if Richard Silver likes you, he pulls out the fifty-year-old cognac at the end of the meal."

"You don't like cognac," I say.

Zoo looks at me as if I am a total dunce. "Trust me, I will find it completely delicious. And you will, too."

We sit together on the sofa.

"Of course if I get the promotion, it means I'll have to work longer hours," he says, sighing, leaning back in the sofa, extending his legs onto the coffee table.

"No," I protest, snuggling closer to him, making an effort to prove to myself that I am still here, still present, that this will all work out, that I will not run naked into the street.

I tell him about my father's employment problems and ask him to look into the company that's threatening to take them over. He promises me he will.

23

He will not play with me because I've banished him from my dreams, although last night, and the last three nights before that, he has tried to sneak in. He wants to know why I don't want him.

I don't want to become my great-grandmother. Or Akka. I don't need his help. I can do this on my own.

Ahh, he says.

I wake up in a panic with a cold, clammy feeling over my body. I toss and turn and wake up tired. I feel ruffled, invaded, guilty, although bits and pieces of dreams stay with me: a mountaintop somewhere in what I imagine are the Himalayas, a bed of rose petals.

Who do I want to be? Good wife, obedient daughter, dispassionate historian, up-and-coming academic? I feel rumblings. Unsteadiness. I feel I am on one of those swinging bridges where all your focus is needed just to stay balanced through all the swaying. I drape my arm around Zoo's waist. He's real. He's here. He might be imperfect, but so am I.

24

I strip all the glossy posters from the walls of my office. All the colorful faces of Ganesh and Parvati and Saraswati with their garlands and pearls and peacock feathers that have enlivened my imagination and my connection to those forces we cannot see or smell or taste. But I must do this on my own. He comes down last. I avoid looking directly into the eyes. I feel guilty sticking him into a box. I have to remind myself it's just a picture. I have to not succumb to superstition and all those aspects of religious belief that have never held any appeal for me.

I face the computer and the chapters of the thesis and their various drafts that sit in neatened piles on my desk. I list the chapters that are completed and the ones that need to be written. The early chapters set the historical stage and seem solid because they are rooted in well-researched historical fact. And then there is Akka, one chapter that has swelled to three. Vanderoe has these sitting on his desk, but I can't hold off until I hear from him; I have to keep pushing ahead. In the five remaining unwritten chapters, I will have to continue to build the case for mystical transformation, delving into the lives of the other saints and making comparative analyses with other religious traditions.

My computer dings me. I see it's an email from Vanderoe.

"Have chapters. In office. Come by."

Should I read hope into the neutrality of the email? No, I won't dare to hope. If he is satisfied, I can be pleasantly surprised. Still, I push my chair back with dread. Walk down the hall cracking my fingers. Telling myself that this is no time to be cowardly. Confidence, girl. The chapters are good. The best I've written. Inspired. He's going to be happy.

I rap on his office door. He's standing by his beautifully organized bookshelves with the book spines all in alphabetical order. His lustrous rosewood desk and the heavy wood filing cabinets are immaculate. He pushes the three chapters across his desk. I pick them up. There are notes scribbled up and down the margins. I squint to read his handwriting, struggle to understand his objections. He's still insisting on much more minutia of information: more facts, more statistics, more evidence. Not only is he demanding more, he has scratched big 'X's over large portions. Rage stings me.

"I can't write this." I hold the pages up.

"You might be better off over in the literature department," Vanderoe says mildly.

I stare at him. I can't believe he's just said what he's said. "Start all over in a new department? That's ridiculous."

"I don't approve of the direction you're going. It's simply not scholarly enough. If we want the academic world to take our work seriously, we have to give it a scientific basis." More than telling me this, he growls it.

"Since when has the study of world religions been under the sciences?"

Vanderoe sits in his ample swiveling desk chair. "It's your choice. Go ahead and write it the way you want; I just can't guarantee I'll pass it."

I stare at him in disbelief. Speechless. What I'm trying to do, I want to scream at him, is write a historical thesis that has passion. I refuse to write about mystic poets as if they were lab results for a drug test.

He picks up his phone. Conversation over.

I rush over to Duck's office, knocking frantically on her door, trying the handle, finding it locked. I forget that she's away to give a talk in San Francisco. I even try Louis' office, but it, too, is dark and locked. I return to my own office, ready to pack it in. Quit. Join Rebecca's lawsuit. Blow up the whole building. Anything but carry on with this farce.

I throw the chapters I'm holding in my hand onto the desk. I reach for my purse and back out of the office. Race to get outside. Run as far as I can. Students are leaning into a strong wind, wrapped in wool coats and winter scarves, carrying loads of books. Quit, I want to scream at them. Quit now, while you can.

The traffic thickens around the entrance gates of the University. I weave between the cars to get across. I don't want to go to the apartment. I don't know where to go. My breath is short and my heart races. I think I see a man with a blue hat down the street. Somehow he's responsible for this, the mess I'm in.

Nails, Nails, Nails. I've passed the salon almost every day as I walk up and down Amsterdam to Columbia and home again, never giving a thought to getting a manicure or a pedicure. This time, I don't think twice. I swing open the door, bells jingle, and I step into the smell of alcohol and nail paint. I can escape in here. My failures weigh on me. Self-delusions. Wasted time. I remember Damiana Silver's elegant nails. The perfection of her smile. The strands of her hair glued in place. If only I could be her.

There is one woman at the front counter and two more behind short-legged worktables. They look at me with bored faces. I am the only customer.

"What you want?" The one behind the counter asks, pointing to a long menu of items.

I read anxiously. It's like a foreign language. French tip, UV gels, tips overlay, silk, airbrush.

"I just want a manicure," I say.

"Choose color," she barks.

I look over a rainbow of colors. How will I ever choose? I feel a blast of warm air on my back. Panic. I don't turn to look. Failure there, too. There are the blues. Turquoise. Creamy. Iridescent. His look haunts me. The way he asked for devotion. The way I got sucked into it. What did Vanderoe say? *It's simply not scholarly enough.* I choose a pearly pink.

The skinny one behind one of the booths waves me over. She is the youngest of the three and must get the cheap jobs.

I take my coat off and set my purse on the floor. The girl takes my hands and sticks my fingers into a bowl of warm water. I feel safe with her. She wears no makeup, and her fingernails look as untended as mine. I notice a small cross hanging on a chain around her neck. It's simple, silver-plated. She can't be more than twenty-years old, yet her skin has odd pockmarks here and there, and she has already yawned three times. Each time she says 'sorry' and covers her mouth.

A short man in a leather jacket walks in with a proprietary air and parks himself at the counter. He and the girl behind it exchange a fast conversation in Vietnamese. She hands over a ledger book, he reads it, flipping through a couple pages, and says something and leaves.

"Bastard!" says the woman behind the desk.

"Cocksucker!" says the other woman.

The manicurist pulls my hands out of the water. "They use very bad language," she says.

"Is he the owner?" I ask.

The two other manicurists carry on in Vietnamese, and even without understanding I know it's the old battle: peon versus boss. I feel for them. Vanderoes are everywhere.

"He not good man. He cheat us. I got kid, you know. My husband get laid off. My father sick with cancer."

"I'm sorry," I tell her, feeling a wave of guilt. Her problems put my own into perspective. Still, Vanderoe's words persist and sting like barbed thorns. *Maybe you should be in the literature department.*

"What's your name?" I ask the girl.

"Le Ly," she says. "Lot of cuticle," she tsks, digging away at the filmy buildup of skin around my nails. She misses, and the sharp points of the scissors dig into my finger. A small spurt of blood appears.

"Sorry, so sorry!" she exclaims. She reaches for a cotton ball, soaks it in some antiseptic, and presses it against the wound.

"It's okay," I say, forgiving her instantly. The sharp pain almost feels good. Bolsters my anger and my despair.

She files the nails, asking me if I want square or round. Round, please. She shapes the nails into little Roman arches. She buffs and applies an undercoat. I watch her with a religious intensity. I envy her this simple, practical skill. She applies the pale pink color with a light touch. It's delicate and subtle and caps my long brown fingers prettily.

"Happy?" she asks me.

I nod. If only. I leave her with a big tip and promise to return again.

"Next time mani-pedi, okay? I give you nice massage, too!"

I hit the street, still wanting to run. The idea pops into my head to go drag Zoo out of his office. Maybe playing hooky with him will somehow make this mess go away. The fun days of our courtship when we kissed continuously on the ferry to the Statue of Liberty, and even more arduously under the shadow of her torch are too long ago. The train pulls into Zoo's station. I walk with a light step to his office building, take the elevator up thirty-eight flights, enter the vault-like doors of Silver and Gold and announce myself to Sunday Smith, who doesn't hide her surprise.   She is all glammed up, guarding the entry with her all-important headset and her brisk efficiency.

"Can you let Niles know I'm here?"

"I believe he's in a meeting. Is he expecting you?"

I shake my head. "It's a surprise."

Her eyes scrunch up a bit. "It's not his birthday—"

"No."

"Let me see if I can buzz him. Have a seat."

I sit in the plush chairs and eye the array of business magazines and papers. Zoo pops down the cubicle-lined corridor, and the look on his face confirms that I am the last person he expected to see. He pecks my cheek.

"Is everything okay?"

"No," I whisper. "Can we go have a coffee somewhere?"

He looks around to see if he's being watched.   Sunday has her eyes on us. He squeezes my arm. "I'd love to, but I can't. I'm swamped here. Why didn't you call first?"

Ed walks by and stops to greet me.

"Everything okay?" he asks.

"I'm just trying to get Zoo to play hooky."

"How romantic," he says.   He confirms that we are coming for Thanksgiving.

Zoo puts his arm around my shoulder and walks me out the double glass doors.

"Are you leaving?" Sunday quickly calls out.

"Be right back," Zoo says. "Just put my calls on hold."

As we stand by the elevator I think of all those calls on hold.   All the flashing red buttons. Waiting for the troublesome wife to get whisked away on the elevator. Zoo rolls his head around on his neck.

"I'm quitting," I say. "Vanderoe just told me I had to rewrite or leave the department."

"Jesus. Can he really do that?"

"Yes. I think so."

Zoo's phone buzzes. He pulls it out of his pocket and takes the call.

"Oh, Christ," he says into the phone. "Right, right. I'll be there in a minute."

"Shit. We've got a client in crisis. Can we talk about this at dinner?"

The elevator arrives. The down bell chimes. I walk in and turn to face the closing doors. Zoo waves goodbye. I lean back against the wall of the elevator. My stomach lurches as it drops precipitously to the bottom floors.

Back on the subway, underground air blasts my hair around my head. On my left I have a woman reading the *Wall Street Journal*. She has it expertly folded, halved and halved again. She has a nicely cut black suit, her hair is coiffed in a prim flip, and she wears small pearl studs in her ears. On my right I have a man with plenty of flesh to spare. He exhales vigorously. There is a crust of tomato sauce around the edges of the man's lips, and in his hands he holds the half-eaten log of a meatball sub. Standing in front of me is a petite Indian girl with long, thick braids and a Catholic schoolgirl's uniform who artfully balances against her mother's thigh. It's her I focus on. Her mother is wearing a sari and running shoes. The girl's dark eyes pop out of her face, and she has a seriousness of purpose about her. I see the girl's whole lifetime ahead of her, like mine when I was her age, taking blind step after blind step, trying to live out her displaced cultural inheritance, Catholic/Hindu/fast food/curry, dragging that suitcase of misguided notions around like a ball and chain.

I want to scream. I want to be back in that dream and with that poetry that promised exalted love. Reality sits like an elephant on my head.

You can't have your cake and eat it, too. The voice is like a roar in my head. It's his voice. I look around anxiously. Where did it come from? The train rocks all of us forward and back.

"I'm not going there," I say aloud. The little Indian girl looks at me. So does her mother. I shrink back into my seat. Oh god.

The train slows with the approach of the next stop. I squeeze through the standing passengers and get off just as the doors are shutting. If I weren't so on the brink I would be laughing my head off. Since when do gods speak in clichés?

25

Ed and Mary have set a beautiful table for Thanksgiving with china and crystal wineglasses, and a seasonal floral bouquet as a centerpiece. The table has been extended to accommodate twelve, mostly other couples from the office. We've all brought dishes to share. Before we sit down to eat, Ed lays out architectural plans for the remodel of their apartment. It involves turning one of the closets into a baby's room.

"Ed's idea," Mary says, quick to distance herself from the idea of becoming three.

I trace my finger over the little square space with the word *baby* written over it. The space is barely a smudge print on the drawing. It hardly represents the vast implication of change to come. In the two days since Vanderoe slaughtered my pages I've imagined every possible scenario for change. Quitting, protesting, ignoring, and running away. If having a baby could solve the problem, I'd do that, too. But pregnancy and Ph.D.s are not mutually incompatible. Zoo has counseled me to both quit and stick to my guns. Big help.

Zoo teases Ed and Mary about having children, about

how that will be the end of our friendship, how other couples that have had children enter what seems like forced internment. I walk away from him. If I don't I might pick another argument. We've had three, including one just before coming over here about whether I could skip out of Thanksgiving altogether. I didn't want to come, but Zoo yelled at me to get off my sorry ass, stop sulking, and suck it up. He's right, and I know it, but I don't want him to know it.

When we sit for dinner, Ed wants us to each take a turn and say what we are thankful for, and it can't be the obvious, like how lucky we feel not to be served our meal in a soup kitchen. Mary groans, but he insists. He starts it off.

"I'm thankful I have good friends in my life," he says, lifting his glass and looking at Zoo and me. "And for Mary, of course."

"I'm thankful that pastel colors have gone out of fashion because I'm sick of them and they suck on me," Mary says.

We laugh. Around the table different forms of gratitude are expressed mostly for good food and good friends.

"I'm thankful for the Chinese and Indian economies, which one day will save all our asses," Zoo says.

"For enemies," I say, "who make us sharpen our knives."

"What the hell does that mean?" Ed asks.

Zoo groans. "The ongoing Ph.D. drama."

I have to explain my battles with Vanderoe.

"Academia makes Wall Street look like a bunch of ninnies," someone says.

"I'm starved," Mary says impatiently so we break into

our bread. Ed has roasted a turkey to a brown and crisped perfection, and there is stuffing and mashed potatoes and gravy and cranberry sauce, and I have brought roasted winter vegetables and garlicky green beans to add an Indian touch.

The talk turns to office politics. There is gossip about the various VPs and their stick personalities. Someone mentions that Silver's wife, Damiana, used to be a Playboy Bunny. No way, someone says. I'm sure by the end of the evening someone will have Googled her to prove the point. Zoo mentions that we have been invited to dinner. There's a lot of hooting and hollering.

"You're getting a promotion," Ed says.

"No way," Zoo says, trying to be modest.

"Ed's too nice," Mary says. "He doesn't know how to get ahead." The meanness of her tone silences the table momentarily.

"I assure you, Ed will get a promotion," Zoo says. "He's a thousand times smarter than I am. And furthermore, this thing is just a friendly dinner, probably a thank you because I brought in Gen Med Tech."

I look at Zoo. "Isn't that the company that's trying to take over the company my father works for?"

"How do I know?" Zoo says, blank.

"Because I asked you to look into it for him."

"Think the deal's already gone through, darling. But Daddy should be fine. Gen Med's solvent. Shouldn't be too many layoffs."

Someone changes the subject, and I find myself silently stewing again. Now Zoo is added to the list of enemies for whom

I must sharpen my knives. My plate is overfull with food, and I methodically work my way through the mounds of potatoes and bread stuffing and yams and beans and turkey meat dripping with gravy. I overeat with a sense of mission. I want to fill the hungry animal that is gnawing at my insides. The time I spent with Akka, with the lover, I felt whole, alive. I hardly had to eat, and I was fed. Now that I'm stuffed with the bounty of the autumn harvest, and I've eaten much more than my stomach can possibly hold, I see that one pain cannot mask another pain. *You can't have your cake and eat it, too.*

26

There you are!" Jangles exclaims. "Haven't seen you in a blue moon."

I've almost walked past her without noticing. Her voice calls me out of my frenzied thoughts. I stop. She's so genuinely happy to see me. Her face is radiant and smiling.

"Everything okay?" she asks.

I tell her I'm ready to adopt cows. All of a sudden it seems the right thing to do. The only thing to do.

"Changed your mind?" She looks at me curiously before reaching into one of her bags. She pulls out the notebook. "Pick anyone you like."

"I don't care. They're all good." I don't want to adopt just one cow, I want to adopt ten. Maybe twenty. Maybe a herd of a hundred.

"I can show you my favorite." She flips the page to an undeniably winsome calf with big perky ears and brown dapples.

"Okay," I say. I flip the page. "This one, too. And this one. And this one."

"That's gonna be fifty dollars a month. You sure you

want to do that?"

"I'm positive." What's fifty a month? Nothing compared to what we spend on clothes and lamps and upscale restaurants.

Jangles sighs. She hands me a form to fill out. Name, address, phone, email—that kind of thing.

"Something going on with you?" she asks me as I blacken the form with my personal information.

I look at her. She looks concerned. Thoughts jumble in my head. I stand there mute. Where would I begin? And why? Except she's so loving. So motherly.

"No. I'm fine."

"Okay. If you say so." She hands me five slightly beat up 8x10's of my newly adopted cows.

I will go home and tape them on the refrigerator.

She grabs my arm. "You can come visit my church, you know. If you feel the need." She looks me deep in the eyes. She hands me a card with "Church of the Eternal Good Word" printed on it with an address and phone number. I tuck it into my pocket.

"Thank you," I tell her, backing away from her, afraid of all she seems to be able to see in me.

27

Zoo tells me I better change my mood *pronto*. We're in the taxi on the way to the Silvers' for the long-awaited dinner. I know I must make a decision, but it hasn't come to me. I stare out at the street: at trees now strung up with Christmas lights, shoppers walking with missionary purpose down the avenues, carrying bags filled with what-all. An older woman lists heavily to her right side. A whole family of four, the father leading with the older daughter skipping by his side and the mother lagging behind with the young son. Several businessmen on the run home. A couple of college students with long woolen scarves noosed around their necks. They've all figured it out, I think. Why can't I?

Zoo takes my hand. "Fuck Vanderoe," he says, as if he's been reading my mind. "I'm gonna get this promotion, make a shitload of money; I'll support both of us; I don't have a problem with that."

It angers me to hear him suggest what is a very generous offer. I pull my hand away sharply.

"What am I supposed to do, sit around and make our

apartment beautiful? Get pregnant. Have babies. Make the folks happy. Throw the last five years in the trash?"

"No one's asking you to do that."

The taxi pulls up to a stately East Side tower.

"Here we are. Take a deep breath," Zoo says.

I pull myself together. Stop feeling sorry for myself. Must do this for Zoo. He takes my hand and leads me past the doorman, to the reception desk, where our names are checked and we are waved to the elevator. Penthouse suite.

Dinner with Damiana and Richard Silver goes like this: Gasp at breathtaking view of East River. Admire their Christmas tree, freshly installed and decorated by their interior designer. The theme is "An Old-Fashioned Christmas," the ornaments are handblown glass, each encasing different Currier and Ives winter scenes, snow sledding, duck hunting, Christmas caroling, candle lighting.

Damiana tells me they have been made in a limited edition, and she feels so lucky to have gotten them at all.

"It's so beautiful," I murmur, taking in the carefully designed tableau.

Damiana and Richard are dressed casually in corduroys and cashmere sweaters. Zoo has stuck with the standard suit and tie, and I feel safe enough in a white silk blouse accessorized with a green paisley patterned Indian silk scarf. My hair is tied back in a glittery red and green hair wrap, in tune with the season. I went back to Le Ly and had my nails done again. It didn't taken long for them to chip and fray.

Damiana has a slight cold, a nuisance more than anything she tells us. Richard is a lean and elegant man who doesn't smile easily. He controls facial muscles and gains power. We settle down with drinks and have a heated discussion about what else? The Economy. Bull and bear. Predictions about the recovery of the market. A more Keynesian approach is necessary. Slowly but surely. This is mostly between Zoo and Richard and Damiana. Richard is very angry about corporate fraud. Without the trust of the common stockholder there is no economy.

Zoo boldly states that there's a rumor flying around the office that Damiana was a Playboy Bunny. Damiana breaks out in laughter.

"It's true, it's true. But I also have a law degree."

Richard pats her on the hand. "Couldn't run the business without her."

Zoo has successfully broken the ice.

"And what do you do?" Damiana asks. All eyes on me.

"She's a Classics Scholar," Zoo chimes in before I can formulate a clear sentence that can make its way out of the dark labyrinth of my current doubt.

"Greek or Latin?" Damiana asks.

"Sanskrit," I reply.

"How fabulous!"

Damiana says she feels connected to India, she doesn't know why, and she hopes to travel there one day. I feel myself disappearing in all this elegant opulence. I feel small in the chair, and I re-cross my legs and push myself to sit straighter and feel taller. I wish I had different clothes, more stylish, and higher heels. I feel the weight of all my un-achievements all over again. Have I ever hated myself more?

Richard returns the talk to corporate doings. He quizzes Zoo on his opinions of different stock values. It's Zoo's turn to shine. Much will depend on his answers.

"I wonder if you could do me a favor," Damiana asks, placing her hand on my arm. "Richard doesn't think I should be asking you this—," and she glances at Richard and smiles, and Richard shrugs helplessly, "but I have this beautiful sari that a friend brought me from India, and I was wondering if you could show me how to wear it?"

"Of course. I'd love to," I say.

I follow Damiana down the hallway, through the formal dining room, through the kitchen, where I am introduced to Alberto, the butler. Damiana lets him know that we will sit for dinner in ten minutes or so, and he nods softly. I follow her into what must be their bedroom, and like the rest of the apartment, it looks like a photo layout from *Architectural Digest*. The bed has a luxurious, thick tapestry coverlet on it, and the pillows look as crisp and starched as ones you would find in a luxury hotel. We enter Damiana's walk-in closet, and when she turns the light on I am in awe of the lineup of clothes and coats and shoes and handbags, all arranged by color and length or whatever category distinguishes one item from the next. The sari is hanging by itself from a hanger. It is a gorgeous pink-hued silk with a deep-green border woven with gold thread. The pink reveals a hidden green side depending on which way the material flexes in the light.

"I want to wear it to the Winter Ball," Damiana says, "but I'm really nervous. I don't want to make a fool of myself."

She shows me the matching blouse she had made in one of the tailoring shops in Little India. I leave her in the closet to put the petticoat and blouse on, and go wait in the bedroom.

"It's so good of you to do this. I can't tell you how much I appreciate this," she calls out to me.

"I'm happy to," I say, wondering now if this is why we were invited to dinner, and not, as Zoo thinks, to be vetted for a promotion. It would be a cruel joke on him. I peek into the bathroom with its gleaming black-and-white marble tile and thick, luxurious towels, with the initials RS and DS beautifully embroidered in big gold stitching at the bottom of each one. I walk over to the heavy curtains and pull them aside and see that the bedroom shares the same astounding view as the living room. I sit carefully at the edge of the bed and take in the room. The light, classical string quartet music that was so pretty in the living room plays in here, too. There are photos of Richard's children on the highly polished antique bureau, and other photos of Richard and Damiana together, one of them kissing. Where do they hide their books, I wonder? Knitting? Golf videos? Chia pets? There's no sign of any personal effects. I know this is what Zoo wants. All this. This life.

I want to throw myself through their window and hurl through space to all those floors below. I feel so tired. I don't want to do this anymore. I remember someone saying it takes far more energy to wear a mask. I lie back on the bed and close my eyes.

What would *he* tell me to do? I fall into the deep blackness of silence. It's so comfortable there, so peaceful. Then his voice comes to me. *Know me*, he says.

My eyes flutter open. Damiana is standing above me, looking at me.

I startle up to standing. I flush with embarrassment.

"I'm so sorry," I stutter, smoothing the cover where I lay down.

"No, it's fine. You're tired. It's the season. It's so exhausting."

I mumble that I'm up against a deadline for my thesis. Damiana has the petticoat on, a simple white cotton underskirt that reaches to just above her ankles. She hands me the sari, lets it unravel on the plush carpet. She complains about all the tiny buttons on the blouse and the too-small buttonholes.

She has not tied the petticoat tight enough around her waist.

"If you don't tie this tight enough," I tell her, gathering myself, acting professorial and in charge, "the whole six yards can come undone."

"How humiliating that would be," she says. She sucks her belly in.

What's humiliating, I think as I tighten the drawstring around her narrow waist, pinching until her belly flesh rolls over the top of it, not giving her the slightest bit of slack, is being caught lying down on your husband's boss's bed.

"Ouch," she says.

I carefully tuck one end of the sari into the petticoat,

begin the wrapping process, explaining each step as I go, pleating the silk in the middle, and tucking all the folds into the petticoat. Then I undo it all and have her practice.

Richard's voice booms out over the intercom. "D," he calls her. "How's it going in there?"

"He must be starving," she whispers. "Give me another minute," she calls out sweetly and practices the whole wrapping procedure another time. She seems to have a natural skill, and it looks credible.

"I want to show this to Richard before I take if off," she says, and we walk back down the series of hallways and through the kitchen where Alberto mentions that dinner is ready to be served and into the living room where Damiana does a slow turn in front of the boys.

"Fantastic," Richard says, as he looks over Damiana.

Zoo adds in his compliments. He tells me he wishes I would wear a sari more often. I look at him incredulously.

Richard walks over to his wife and kisses her.

"The Winter Ball, what do you think?" she asks.

"You'll make a splash," he says. "But I'm hungry. How about some chow?"

"I'll go change," Damiana says quickly.

Richard moves Zoo and I into the elegant and formal dining room. The walls are done in deep-red silk brocade. The table is set with a centerpiece of holly and white gardenias. A soft candle glows in the middle. Damiana rushes in, slightly breathless, and takes her place opposite Richard.

"What a relief to have that petticoat off!" she exclaims.

I laugh and tell her it's why I almost never wear a sari.

The four of us occupy only one end of the table.

We clink crystal wine goblets with a toast to a wonderful upcoming holiday season with a special hopeful murmur for peace. Alberto, crisply uniformed in black and white, serves courses.

French: simple and refined. Vichyssoise. Creamy and flavorful. Coq au vin. Haricots Verts, Salade Frisée. Everything perfect.

The Winter Ball is for Damiana's favorite charity— Historic Preservation Society of New York. She and Richard are chairs of this year's event.

"I would love it if you both would come," she says. "It's very fun, actually, even though it sounds stuffy."

We murmur that we would love to.

Alberto clears the plates thankfully and returns with dessert. Chocolate soufflé.

We retire to the living room. Out comes Alberto with a bottle of cognac and four snifters. I look at Zoo. He smiles.

"What a lovely evening," Zoo says, taking my hand. He is slightly giddy. Intoxicated with the smell of his promotion.

I hate him even as I smile and agree and slip my hand out of his.

The taxi is downstairs.

"Thank you so much for everything!"

"We'll do it again," Damiana says.

"We'll have you over for some Indian," Zoo offers boldly.

I can't imagine them coming over to our badly in need

of repair apartment.

"I love lamb saag and that rice dish, what is it called?"

"Biryani?"

"Yes! Do you make that?"

"Yes, certainly."

"Oh, you'll have to teach me."

"With pleasure."

"You were an absolute angel for teaching me how to wear the sari. I hope I will remember."

"You will. I can help you before the ball, if you'd like."

"Oh, would you?"

"Certainly." I can't believe I've made the offer. Acting like I'm her best friend.

Hand clasps with Richard, much warmer than when we entered. Kisses with Damiana.

Laughter,

Elevator,

Air.

28

Zoo wants to know if he was good. He hangs up his suit and we switch into our pajamas. I let all my clothes pile onto the floor.

"Yes," I tell him. "You were good."

Zoo comes and hugs me from behind. "What a fucking view, eh?"

I slip out of his arms.

"How'd it go in there with you and Damiana and the wrap-around thing? You were gone an awfully long time."

"Fine." I don't want to tell him how I was caught lying down on their bed. He will rip into me.

"You were quiet," Zoo says.

I climb into bed and dig myself in under the covers. "I'm tired." His voice is still in my head. *Know me.* Is that the answer? How can it be?

Zoo climbs in next to me. "I don't know. I'm not sure. He's such a weasel, you know, ultimately."

I don't respond.

"Anjali, are you listening to me?"

"Who's a weasel?"

"Silver. But he did bring out the cognac."

"That's what you wanted, right?" Along with the butler, the interior decorator, and the magic vacuum cleaner that sucks up any sign of human life.

"Damn right."

I pull the covers all the way to my chin. I close my eyes. *Know me*, he said. I have abandoned him. But he has not abandoned me.

29

When I walk into my office I shove my thesis aside and work on some translations for Duck. I hardly look up from my computer for most of the morning. Duck often comes to the university on Saturdays, so I decide to check her office around noon. My plan is to appeal to her to intervene with Vanderoe.

Her light is on. She's dressed casually, almost frumpy, in jeans and a sweater. We have had some of our best work sessions on Saturdays when the halls are quiet and the phone barely rings.

"Read this," she commands, barely saying hello, and hands me some pages.

"Before we talk about this, I need to ask you something—"

She raises her eyebrows.

"I need a new adviser. I can't work with Vanderoe. He's threatened to fail me if I don't change my thesis."

"Aachh," Duck says, spewing a guttural complaint. Her face is full of disgust, and I feel hopeful.

I fill her in on the latest conversations.

Duck shakes her head. "It's too late. It's just too late in the game now. You'll practically have to start over."

"I'll quit working for you, then you can be my adviser."

"Oh no. I need your translations. I can't let you do that. I won't."

My heart sinks. "I can't do it his way."

"You have got to finish it. There's just no discussion about that."

"Do you want to see his notes? Can I show them to you?"

"It won't do any good. I can't interfere."

"The thing is, I've finally hit my stride. I know what I'm writing now. I can't turn it into a bunch of statistics notes. Someone like Dr. Veeraswamy understands completely what I'm doing."

"Unfortunately he is at a university in California."

Duck sits down at her desk. "Let me tell you something." She instructs me to sit down.

"You aren't going to win this battle. Vanderoe's got a lot of clout. He's an ass, a powerful one. Pretend. Act. Do what you have to do. Play the game. You'll be able to do plenty of important work the rest of your life. For now, you need to find a way to do what he wants."

I stare at her speechless. Why is this so hard for me now? All my life I've been playing the game. I should be expert at it.

"Brihadaranyaka Upanishad." Duck's Sanskrit is impeccable. "Look at what it is saying!"

I read the pages Duck handed me. She stands behind me, peering over my shoulder. It's a conversation between Yājñavalkya, a rishi, a wise and ancient teacher, renowned for his imperious manner, and Gargi, a female theologian and an accomplished weaver.

Gargi is one of the most learned and sharp students of life.

Yājñavalkya, she says, if the waters are the weft on which this whole universe is woven, on what weft are the waters woven?

On the wind, Gargi.

What weft is it then on which the wind is woven?

On the worlds of the atmosphere, Gargi.

What weft is it then on which the atmosphere is woven?

Yājñavalkya patiently answers each question, knowing all along the trap Gargi is trying to lead him into.

Finally Gargi asks: What weft is it then, on which the worlds of the Creator are woven?

Yājñavalkya lets her have it. *Disciple, do not question too much or your head will fall off. You are asking too many questions about a deity about which too many questions should not be asked!*

"It smacks of fascism, don't you think?" Duck says impatiently.

"It's exactly how I feel with Vanderoe," I say glumly.

"Yes, but what the old bastard really is saying, is don't even ask. Don't even ask! It's bad for the health, you see. It's not 'I don't know or it is not knowable.' It's 'shut up or risk losing your head.' You can't know it in the way of traditional knowledge—you have to know it in the way of faith."

"But if it is just faith, it can't ever be proven to be true."

"Of course not," Duck says. "And it doesn't need to be proven in a scientific way. Scientific truths can be communicated, but religious truths can't be. They can only be understood through experience."

I look at Duck for a moment, absorbing what she has just said. Of course she's right. There is no way to prove or disprove the love Akka had for Shiva, or any divine experience for that matter. It just is.

"Hurry up with the work I gave you. I haven't got forever," she says, stepping back to her chair.

"Right." I will have to play the game and have it my way, too.

30

I pick up my thesis. Take a deep breath. Think like Vanderoe. Add statistics. Scientific explanations. That isn't the hard part. What kills me is giving in to him. Making Akka Mahadevi a historical moment. She has become my big sister. I whisper her poem.

> *Like the circus monkey*
> *and the puppet on the end of a string*
>
> *I've played as you made me play*
> *I've lived as you made me live*
>
> *Until you, my lord white as jasmine,*
> *charioteer of the whole world*
>
> *said*
> *Stop!*

Charioteer of the world. I bring her lover out of the box where I've hidden him. His beautiful face smiles at me. I need his help, and I'm not going to resist him any longer. I will know him, and he will know me. His eyes tell me so.

Duck has shown me how he came to me. Not through the power of reasoning. Not through study and scholarship. He came on a call I didn't even know I made. He is more powerful than Vanderoe, the mere human. I am flirting with danger; I know that. Akka knew what it would take. I'm just a novice. Navigating gods and mortals.

I feel his energy swell up in me. He doesn't jump out of the poster—how silly that I ever feared this. He doesn't have to. I breathe deeply, and I lay the two sets of chapters about Akka in front of me: one a clean copy from my computer and the other with Vanderoe's scrawl over them. Each chapter, I decide, will have two parts. The "scientific" annotations will appear in the second part, separated from the narrative of a young poet searching for the perfect love. One part won't pollute the other part. It will be a dualistic approach, mirroring one of the great arguments in Hindu philosophy. Is the divine separate or within? In my thesis, they will be separate. In my heart, within.

31

Zoo calls me to tell me that he got the promotion. Before I can even say congratulations, or try to show my excitement for him, or ask him how we are going to celebrate, he tells me he will be home late; he's going out to party with the boys.

"Good," I say. "Have a good time. You deserve it."

"This is it, baby," he says. "This is it."

When I return home, I find the black stone lingam I purchased in Chicago. I clear a space for an altar on the nightstand next to my bed. I set the lingam along with the Ganesh and the Saraswati on an Indian paisley print textile saved from my undergrad days. Next to it I set the incense burner, and I light a small candle in the diwa. I find little talismans I have saved, a shard of pottery found on a trip to a Hopi Reservation, a polished clamshell from Cape Cod, a peace insignia from a college rally. I wish I had known my great-grandmother. Being like her scares me less now than dying the slow death that has been creeping into my bones.

The deep woodsy smell of sandalwood incense perfumes

the air, and the blue smoke drifts in currents through the room. I sit cross-legged on the floor and loosen my mind.

I chant his mantra. *Om Nama Shivaya.* And chanting it, I feel like I'm entering a dark but welcoming place. Each breath tastes like a candy in my mouth. I suck on it, allowing the slowest of dissolves. I chant rhythmically. The chanting takes on a force of its own. My mind pulsates in gentle waves. I lose myself in his name. His energy. I feel a burning sensation in my palms. They hum with a power I didn't know I had in me. Until now.

The key turns in the lock. Zoo calls my name and pulls me out of my meditation. A guilty smile is wedged over Zoo's teeth as he steps into the bedroom.

"Hello, darling. You're not angry with me are you?"

I shake my head no.

"What's with all that incense?" he calls out to me. "I can barely breathe in here."

"Just meditating."

"You're not turning religious on me, are you?"

He walks over to me and lifts me from my sitting position. He swings me around in his arms. He's so happy. I don't want to ruin it. He kisses me.

"You smell delicious," he murmurs as he sets me down and walks to the kitchen. He is excited by his promotion. We toast to his success. He tells me how the promotion came down. Exactly like in the movies. He is summoned into Richard's office. Robert, the other Silver, is there, as are two other VPs. Zoo doesn't know them well. They came onboard when the merger happened. They ask him to sit down. Zoo said he didn't have a clue as to the purpose of the meeting. He scanned his brain to see if one of his accounts was in trouble. Others have been laid off since the merger was announced. Was it his turn? They chitchat for a bit. An ordinary Thursday morning. Finally, Richard breaks the news with a smile. Will he accept Senior VP? A smile! And then they hand him three big accounts.

I listen, but it seems as if Zoo is describing the games of boys.

"We are lucky, aren't we?" he says.

"Yes," I murmur.

"Do you want to have a baby?" Zoo asks, ambushing me. "I mean, do you want to try?" His voice is low, almost embarrassed.

He pulls me like a rag doll towards the bedroom. I acquiesce. This is my weakness.

Take pity on me today,
Lord,
exile my greed
and show me the way out

Zoo does not think of stock prices, and I do not think of my heart's greed. I let Zoo taste the spice of my desire; the sweet sweat of my devotion even though I know it has been cooked up in the heat of the Other. Our reckless abandon leaves us whipped, sated, and awe-struck.

Later, awake, a burden of guilt wraps my heart. His blue skin is on my mind. It's as if I have him next to me, silent, each breath long and deep, as if nothing could be more delicious than the air we drink together. His deliberate breathing slows mine down. He is meditating on something, I don't know what. His hair is damp and moist and smells of a river. I want to touch him. Take him. I am weak with the desire to swim in his very being.

His heat scorches. I throw off all the covers. I get out of bed and draw up the covers around Zoo. In the bathroom I look into the mirror. There he is behind me, smiling. He's following me. I turn to look him in the face. He places a palm against my cheek. I take it down, but he holds my wrist. He draws me near him.

He tells me our work is just beginning.

I look into his eyes. They are clear and bright, as if the full moon shines in them. Beautiful. Rapturous. Enticing.

I walk forward to the bed, and he walks backwards, never loosening his gaze off mine.

32

Christmas is upon us and a sense of dread shadows me. How will we get through the season? How will I, flirting as I am with *'this world and that other,'* as Akka says. *Husband inside, lover outside. I can't manage them both.* Zoo and I are both working like salmon swimming upstream in the spawning season. Every morning gone early, bags under the eyes, every evening home late, neck stiff, shoulders slumped. There is no time to be tuned into each other's moods or weird turns of mind.

Zoo begs me to buy the tree this year before he leaves for work early one morning. With only a week left to go, the pickings will be slim. Intrepid salesmen have set up shop on many street corners. Their prices are exorbitant. I pass the trees every day, the aromatic smell of their fir following me home.

I politely suggest we skip the whole tree business and limit our giving to one special gift apiece. Our closets are already overcrowded with Christmases past. Zoo looks like he has been stabbed in the ribs just above his diaphragm. Christmas, to him, is an affirmation of the one guaranteed moment of happy times from his childhood. His parents went all-out on this one holiday, celebrating in their country home near the coast. Apparently, there used to be mountains of presents under a towering tree. I have visions of Fat Boy tearing through box after box, insatiable in his appetite for more.

My family, on the other hand, celebrated a grinch version of Christmas. Not from stinginess really, more from being clueless. A great show of opulence is not the Indian way. Nita and I protested. One year we won the small victory of an artificial tree and one present each. We longed for what everyone else had, a sense of belonging to a time and a place.

I promise Zoo I will do the tree, but he must try to be circumspect on the gift giving.

"Fine," he says, rushing out the door.

On the way home from the university that evening, I stop and examine the choices that have been decimated by our waiting so long.

"What size you looking for, lady?" the tree salesman asks. He is wearing a bright-red knit hat and a red jacket with white fake-fur trim. All he is missing is the cotton beard.

"Just a small tree. Not more than four-feet tall."

He shuffles through a pile of twine-bound trees. He chooses one and swiftly cuts the string. He shakes it out, and a small tree unravels. I try and see it with Zoo's eyes. He likes his trees full bodied.

I shake my head. "Too skimpy," I say.

"No, lady, when the branches relax, it's gonna be fine."

"Don't you have some others to show me?"

He leans the tree against the building and whips out another. It's not much better. The more he shows me, the pickier I get. One looks lopsided, another anorexic; one doesn't have a pointy top for a star.

As I am fussing, Jangles shuffles by. She's carrying the cardboard pieces she uses to display her wares, and she is weighed down by bags of her merchandise. Our eyes meet, and the odd smile we exchange acknowledges the strange way we are connected in this vast world of wandering souls.

"You gonna get a tree?" she asks.

"Yeah. My husband wants one."

"Jesus' light is coming to town," she says. She smiles. There is genuine anticipation in her eyes. "You ever seen his light?"

"No," I say. "I don't believe I have."

"I'm gonna light a candle. What you gonna do?"

I smile sheepishly. "I don't really believe in this holiday. I mean, I didn't celebrate it growing up. I do it for my husband. I'll cook a nice meal."

The tree seller holds up another one for me.

"How much you charging for these trees?" Jangles asks, not altogether nicely.

"If you ain't buying, get lost," he says.

"Where's your Christmas spirit?" she says.

"I got a family to feed," the man says. "You buying or not?" He looks at me. He's impatient now. I've taken a lot of his time.

"No," I say. "But thank you." I walk with Jangles down

the street.

"How are you feeling these days?" I ask her.

"Feeling the cold in my bones," she says. "Feeling like I wish I was someplace else."

"I feel the same way," I say.

"No, you're too young to be feeling that way."

We come to the entrance of my building. I stop. "This is where I live," I tell her.

She wants to know where exactly. I have her count up four floors and over to the corner window.

"I'm gonna look for your candle up there."

"Would you like to come upstairs? Warm up with some hot tea?"

A huge smile erupts over her face. She follows me in. Gene, the doorman, ever watchful for hustlers and lowlifes, raises half an eyebrow.

Jangles stands in our apartment as if she is in the great hall of the Metropolitan Museum. The heat feels luscious after the prickly December cold. My hair flies up as I remove my scarf and jacket. Electric sparks. Jangles is not ready to take her coat off. She stands in front of the radiator and warms her hands. I rush to put the kettle on the stove. Then I make a fire in the fireplace.

"You living some life," she says, scoping out the apartment.

I see it again through the eyes of a poor woman who sells trinkets out of a cardboard stall. The table set for two, the plush furniture, the large-screen television. It's embarrassing.

When the water boils, I make tea in a pot and set a plate of treats on the coffee table. She seems to enjoy her tea immensely and isn't shy about helping herself to the cookies, but it is the caramel popcorn that she really seems to relish.

"You happy here?" she asks me. "Ain't my business but—"

"I'm happy enough," I say.

"Happy enough, I like that," she says. She looks at me with a skeptical glance. "I get this feeling, see, that you ain't going to be here forever."

"I didn't know you were a fortune teller," I say, teasing.

"I'm not," she says. "When you cross over to that other side, you come back knowing stuff," she says. She waves her hand in the direction of heaven; she rolls her eyes upward.

"What did you see when you were up there?"

"Didn't see a thing. Felt it. Felt grace lay its hand on me." She looks directly at me. She holds her hand to her bosom, the very place where he thumped so hard. Thinking of it brings him back. My own heart starts to beat fast.

"Some folks think I'm crazy. But what I know, I know in my heart."

"I don't think you're crazy," I say. I stutter. "Your heart attack, the other man…"

She looks at me puzzled.

"Can I show you something?"

I lead her into the bedroom, to my little altar. I pick up the lingam and explain to her how it represents Shiva, his creative power, his masculine and feminine aspect: the Shiva and the Shakti. I tell her how he's a complex god who holds both destruction and creation, that he's erotic and ascetic, and all powerful. She looks the lingam over and holds it in her hand reverentially, but I can see it's just an object to her and the scholarly version leaves a blank expression on her face. I want her to understand. So I tell her what happened that day she had the heart attack, and how I've been haunted by the man ever since. I ask her if she remembers the man who looked at the watch and explained why cows are sacred.

"Now you're giving me goose bumps," she says. "He *was* odd."

I tell her one of the dreams. She shakes her head in disbelief. I tell her about Akka Mahadevi and my great-grandmother. How complicated it is. How I'm afraid of what is happening to me.

"I see what you mean," she says, not at all laughing at me. Her face is so kindly with its splotches and odd freckles here and there, her wonderful lump of a nose and her eyes that bring calm wherever she turns her gaze. "I knew something big was going on with you," she says. "Knew it in my bones." She takes my hands in hers. "Nothing wrong with what's happening to you. Nothing at all. One thing I know about life; it isn't simple. You will find your way. Maybe he just came along to help."

I feel relieved, as if a weight has been lifted off me. Not so crazy, and alone. I wonder if I told Zoo this, what would happen. Maybe it's not as hard as I've been making it out to be.

"Can I have more of that tea?" she says. We go back to the living room. I want to know where she grew up and what happened to her. So she tells me. She was born in southern

Ohio in a family of five boys and four girls; her mother and father had a small dairy farm with her grandparents. She tells me she had two children with a man not much more than a boy by the time she was eighteen, but he beat her, so she took the two kids and moved to Cincinnati where she got work as a waitress and singing in a night club and met a white man who wanted to marry her. He gave her a big diamond ring and a white Corvette and she thought she had it made, but then it turned out he drank too much and beat her, too. So she took her kids back to her parents' farm and got on a bus to New York City. She was thirty-two, and she lived with a cousin who got her hooked on junk.

"Wow," I say.

She nods her head up and down. "It's the truth," she says. She lifts one of her pants and shows me needle scars up and down her leg. "I don't want to tell you what that was like," she says. "I don't want to go back there. I did everything in the book, including time in prison."

By now, we are in the middle of our second refill of tea when Zoo enters, his arms full of shopping bags with bright-colored tissues and ribbons and shiny bows peeking over the edges. I jump up from the sofa like a Jack-in-the-Box and feel more incriminated having Jangles here than I would had I been caught with a man in bed.

Zoo stops abruptly, his whole body stiffens, and I can see the puzzlement on his face.

"Zoo, you remember the woman—" I say by way of introduction.

Zoo sets his bags down near the fireplace and nods politely towards Jangles.

"Saved my life," Jangles says, nodding.

"Right," Zoo says. "Tell me your name again?"

"Thelma Boatwright. What you say your name was?" Jangles asks.

"Niles."

"Thought she called you Zoo or something."

I laugh. "That's my nickname for him."

"She calls you Jangles," Zoo says.

Jangles laughs and shakes her arms up and down. Her bracelets clank against each other.

"He makes wonderful animal sounds," I add. "He can do almost any animal you can find in a zoo."

Jangles eyes him curiously as he glares at me. "Can you do an elephant?" she asks.

Zoo stumbles for a moment. Then he purses his lips and lets out a muted shriek.

We laugh. "Not my best," Zoo says. "I'm better with amphibians and the like."

"This some nice place you got here," Jangles says.

"Why thank you," Zoo says.

"Care for some tea?"

"No thanks. No tree yet?" Zoo looks around the apartment as if somehow I might have hidden the tree.

"Just couldn't find the perfect one," I say. "Tomorrow, I promise."

"Don't trouble yourself. I'll go get one right now," Zoo says. He still has his coat on. "You two enjoy your tea and biscuits."

Jangles stands up just as he turns the doorknob. "Pleasure meeting you, sir." She hands Zoo a card. "I'd like it if you came to my church. We read scripture every evening." She smiles just as big a smile as her face will hold.

"Lovely," he says, stuffing the card in his coat pocket, and makes a quick exit.

Jangles reaches for her coat. "I'll be getting on now."

"You don't have to rush out," I say lamely.

"How come you ain't got no dog?" Jangles asks.

I explain that I'm not a dog person and Zoo is too busy.

"Do you have a dog?" I ask her.

"Used to have one named Scrip, for scripture. Little black dog with a yellow tail. I loved that dog like nobody's business," she says.

"Was he a mutt?" I ask.

"Oh yeah," she says. "He had a little bit of everything in him. You got more of that caramel corn? I'll take some to go."

I happily scoop some into a zip-loc bag for her. I accompany Jangles down the elevator and out to the street. The cold blasts us.

"Like I was saying *get a dog*. Dog helps a marriage." Jangles smiles. She wraps her big coat tightly around herself and shuffles on down the avenue.

33

Christmas morning I walk to the windows and see that a light snow is falling, the first of the winter. Zoo adds logs to the fire and prods it until a nice, hot flame shoots up. I wonder what we will be doing a year from now, will anything have changed? Will I not be living here as Jangles has foreseen? The day ahead feels long and empty. The pressure in my head has been building. My nights are restless and sleepless, my days banging against the wall of my thesis. He comes and he goes, flashes of blue, voices that prod me along with cryptic wisdom: *do not be careless about truth, do not think of anything as 'mine,' know me as I am, know me.* The voices push me forward, prod me, and poke me.

Boxes have arrived from overseas. Zoo's mother subscribes to the same philosophy as he does. I know how much it means to him to have a good healthy pile to work through on Christmas morning and, guilt ridden, I joined the hordes. Beyond the usual pajamas and shirts and robot sets, I splurged on an antique watch.

We open presents.

"I do love Christmas," Zoo says.

"I love how everything stops for this week," I say. And I do.

Zoo's mother has sent me lovely potholders with botanical prints and her newest book, a collection of edited articles on gardening with native plants. She has sent Zoo three cashmere sweaters, flannel pajamas, and a newly released history of the British Empire and its decline. Nita has sent us a gift certificate to a hot new Brazilian restaurant. Zoo tells me he has a special gift for me. He's saving it for last.

He opens the box with the watch and flips out. Its big black face with inlaid mother-of-pearl and old leather watchband looks elegant on his wrist. He claims it's the very thing he's been wanting. I smile and say I'm so happy. Everything between us feels phony and forced.

I can't imagine what he has up his sleeve for me.

Finally we're left with a pile of torn-up wrapping papers and emptied boxes and Louis Armstrong crooning Christmas carols. We slump in the sofa.

"Jangles said she didn't see me living here much longer," I tell Zoo.

Zoo looks surprised. "Wow, maybe she is telepathic or something. Come on. Get your coat on. We're going on a little field trip. Dress warm. We're walking."

"Now?"

"Yeah, now. Want your Christmas present or not?"

We're smacked with cold December air and set off, Zoo leading, me following. The streets are virtually empty. It is one of those winter days without sun, the sky a dingy gray that makes you want to stay in bed, the city almost comatose. The snowflakes are small and roundish and sting when they hit. Only the pigeons strut about with any energy. And Zoo. He takes me by the gloved hand and strides across Central Park like a man on a wartime mission. There are a few lone kids in the park relishing the first snowfall.

I can't think of anything I've said I wanted so I can't imagine where we're headed. We walk deep into the East Side to what looks to be a newly built apartment residence called the Eastport. It towers above all the other buildings on the block, one of those steel-and-glass obelisks that reflect the moods of the sky. Inside, the lobby is done up in muted mauve and gray colors, and the furniture is sleek and black.

"Are we visiting someone?" I ask. I'm deeply confused.

Zoo pushes me towards the elevators and tells me to wait there for him. He whispers something to the uniformed man at the reception desk. It's all very mysterious and baffling. He joins me at the elevators and grins.

"Hope you're ready for this," he says.

"How can I be ready when I have no idea—"

In the elevator the panel displays numbers that ascend to thirty-six, then penthouse. Zoo pushes the button for twenty-five. There's a whoosh and then the fast lift of the elevator and the feeling of my stomach dropping is both real and the result of the tumult of apprehension that is overtaking me. We exit to a long corridor and rows of blank-faced gray doors. I trail Zoo down the carpeted hallway until he stops at apartment number

2575 and produces a key from his pocket and unlocks a double-barreled bolt.

Dread overcomes me. Zoo covers my eyes with his hands and walks us into the apartment.

"Merry Christmas, darling," he says, uncovering my eyes and standing back with an enormous smile on his face.

"This is ours. What do you think?"

I take in the empty sweep of gleaming wood floor that butts into a bank of tall windows. The living room could easily house two different seating arrangements with big sofas and chairs. The ceiling is high and white; and everywhere the lines are clean and crisp. We walk over to the windows and take in the view that looks south down First Avenue, clotted with uneven rooftops, through to bits of the river and the bridges that cross over to Brooklyn and Queens.

Zoo turns me to take in the kitchen. "Imported Italian cabinets," Zoo says, and he goes over and starts opening doors and inside are revealed layers of shelves and handy organizers. The drawers glide open noiselessly. One soft touch and they close on their own. The countertop is a thick expanse of polished black granite. And he shows me an under-counter wine refrigerator and hidden pull-out cabinets for trash.

"It's just so fucking cool, isn't it?" he says.

And then we're off to the master bedroom. The emptiness of the space makes our footsteps echo. Another crisp expanse that shares the same view as the living room. Zoo maps out where the bed will go and imagines that we can have a large flat-screen television mounted on the wall and lets me know the whole apartment is pre-wired for audio. A sliding door that blends in seamlessly with the wall opens to reveal a large walk-in closet. Not as big as Damiana Silver's but close enough. And the bathroom is mirrored and tiled and shiny and clean with two sinks and a shower that hides behind a sheer wall of glass. And there's more: two more twin-sized bedrooms, cozy and square that share their own bathroom.

"Baby's room," Zoo says, and I stare into the blank space, numb. "And room for your parents to visit."

"Why did you do this?" I ask, tucking my hands deep into my coat pockets.

"Are you kidding me?" he says. "You don't like it?" He looks at me for the first time; he's been so involved with his own enthusiasm.

"I don't want to move. I'm happy where we are."

"This is why I don't tell you things," he says angrily. "You just oppose me."

I can see his hurt and frustration with me. I don't want to be a ball and chain on his happiness.

"Doesn't this mean more debt? Isn't this stupid with the way the economy is going?"

"I think I know what I'm doing, Anjali. It's not like I'm stupid about money."

I look around again. The barren walls. The rooms to be filled with carpets and sofas and chairs and tables and lamps and meaningful artwork.

"We'll do it all in white," Zoo says. "White shag rug, white Italian leather sofas, I want white everywhere."

"*Fait accompli*," I say, walking back over to the monstrous windows, staring out into the thickening eddy of snow.

34

T he walk back through the park feels like a minefield. One false step and the whole hidden façade of the marriage is going to blow up. My heart races. It's cold outside, but it was colder in that apartment. I would rather be buried in the white blanket of snow than the white tomb of that apartment. Footsteps are being erased almost as quickly as they are made. I walk fast to catch up with Zoo who is about ten paces ahead; I tell Zoo that I am not moving into the apartment. He turns to look at me with torpedo eyes.

"Here are the facts, darling. I've already put a substantial non-refundable cash deposit. Let me repeat. Non-refundable. If you weren't so insistent on being pigheaded and spoiled," he tells me, "you would see that this is a very good move. The price has been substantially lowered. Now is the time to buy. It's a very good investment whereas continuing to shell out a lot of cash on a funky old apartment that sooner or later is going to need a hell of a lot of structural repair is just shortsighted and stupid."

"Feel free to move there by yourself," I tell him. I can

hardly believe I say it. But I do.

"Oh my god," he screams. "This is so fucking ridiculous. What has happened to you? Have you gone off your rocker? Who are you?"

"I could ask you the same question," I scream back.

And then we have to check our screaming because we pass a group of carolers making their way across the park. They wear Santa hats and are swinging little golden bells and are red faced and laughing and scooping up snow and throwing it at each other. Seeing them, I feel doubly betrayed.

"I didn't realize," I say, as soon as we pass out of earshot of the carolers, "that you made all the decisions, and I am just conveniently to go along."

"Oh my god, is this what this about? You want to turn this into a power game?"

"Marriage is supposed to be about partnership."

"Marriage is looking out for one another. I'm doing my part. That's how I see it. I'm looking out for our future."

"You're looking out for your own future. Because you never consulted me on what I want my future to look like."

We arrive back at our own apartment, and I feel desperate to go somewhere else, but it is Christmas, and everyone is busy and happy with their families and thinking of that makes me feel even more imprisoned. We ride the elevator in silence. Dinner is just around the corner, and I had shopped and planned for an elegant Christmas meal, roast Cornish hens with cranberry glaze and potatoes Anna and peppery greens and homemade biscuits and English trifle for dessert.

I get to the cooking and hear Zoo poke around in the fireplace trying to revive what's left of the coals. It's good to have something to do, transforming ingredients into a meal, although the little raw bodies of the two hens make me sad as they sit side by side in the pan all trussed up, salted, peppered, and herbed. I baste them with butter and oil and silently thank them for their sacrifice, and stick the little birds in the oven and then get to slicing potatoes, but my hands are still quivering, and I cut my finger, just a surface cut, but enough to cause a spurt of blood.

As the apartment fills with aromas of food cooking, and the tree twinkles prettily, I remember that I have not put a candle in the window as I promised Jangles I would. Zoo is in the shower. I light a candle and stare out into the night and see that snow is still coming down in a gentle torrent. I should call my parents and Nita, too, but I'm afraid if I do they will read the distress in my voice and want to know what the matter is, or they will ask me what I got for Christmas, at least Nita will, and that will make me divulge the whole story, and Nita will think the new apartment sounds cool and won't understand why every bone in my body is in protest.

Still I set an elegant table with our nice china and silverware and antique candlesticks, and watch Zoo carefully. Maybe he will have a change of heart. Maybe this situation can be salvaged. All I want, really, is for him to consider me, see me, acknowledge my apprehensions, acknowledge that it takes two to make a marriage, that we are not on a hike up Mount Everest where obviously an experienced leader is required; we are simply trying to make a life that can hold our love and the duality of our beings. He pops the cork of a bottle of wine. He is freshly shaved and has put on one of his new cashmere sweaters, a baby-blue one, for our dinner. I go into the bedroom to do the same. When I emerge, Zoo is at the CD player cursing. Something is not working, and he is jabbing at stereo connections and has worked himself into a froth. And then, as if the apartment is conspiring against me, too, all the lights go off. Something has short-circuited in the wiring. I've already lit candles, and Zoo stumbles to the door, cursing, and goes down to the basement to flip the circuit breaker.

I put dinner on the table. When he returns, he's still cursing. "Who would want to leave this beautiful place?" he says, rubbing it in. "Well, Merry Christmas, such as it is," Zoo says as he raises his glass as a toast, and I say, yes, "Merry Christmas."

35

Zoo tells me he must fly off to Brussels for an international monetary conference. His voice is thick with anger. "When?" I ask. As far as I'm concerned, he can't leave soon enough. We have been stomping past each other with our swords drawn for weeks now.

"Tuesday."

Wednesday is our anniversary, but neither of us will mention it. Our February wedding. Our vows given in the traditional Indian style. My parents consulted an astrologer for an auspicious date then went all out and rented a ballroom in a swank Chicago hotel. Mimi and Roger thought the whole idea exotic and wonderful. Zoo refused to arrive on a horse with trumpets blaring, but we did exchange thickly woven flower garlands to acknowledge our life-long bondage to each other. Our hands were tied together to symbolize our union, my hands painted dark with henna, to make the bond nice and strong. Ceremonial marks of turmeric and red *kumkum* powder stained on our foreheads in honor of the gods. Finally, Zoo led me around the sacred fire seven times—his dhoti tied with a knot to my sari

—and with this we were married. The guests showered grains of rice on us to symbolize fertility. It may have been the happiest day of our parents' lives.

But now we have become invisible to each other, like those super-clean glass windows of the new apartment that birds will fly into head on. We haven't spoken much since he bequeathed us with the new apartment. My mind is still reeling between the twin facts that he made what is now an irreversible decision without consulting me, and the sickening thought of myself towering twenty-five stories up suffocating in clinical, maddening whiteness. And it's not even that. It's something fundamental in the way I've been disregarded, overlooked.

I escape into meditation to find peace. I chant his name. Like a good lover, he is kind. He wants to know what troubles me. When I tell him, he listens. He doesn't give me answers. Breathe with me, he says, be with me. It's only in that quiet space that the anger drops away.

But then Zoo and I are right back at it. I ask gently if there isn't a way out of the apartment.

"You have no vision," Zoo screams at me over soup. I have to do all the thinking for this family. You've always got your goddamn nose stuck in some book. Or you're meditating or praying or doing some cock-assed thing like that."

And so I scream back. "You have no clue who I am or what I want because you never bothered to ask me. Maybe I don't want to live like you do."

Before he leaves in the pitch black of Tuesday morning, having packed the night before, he sits next to me on the bed as if I am a sick patient and he the doctor and tells me to please, please trust him on this, that he's doing this for *us*, and he produces a small maroon-colored box and says Happy Early Anniversary, and he opens it because I don't make a move to, and displays a simple strand of lustrous pearls, but even as he shows it to me he knows he cannot penetrate my alienation from him with this empty gesture.

I have no present for him.

"Okay, darling," he says, kissing me lightly on the top of my head. "At least I'm trying, I hope you can see that." He shuts the light by the bed and wheels his suitcase out the door. "By the way," he calls out. "I'll do all the packing when I get back. And moving. You don't have to lift a finger."

There is a terrible silence when the door clicks shut.

36

I stare at the pile of work in the stranglehold of my office, make feeble attempts at translating some particularly obtuse philosophical text that stares back at me with taunting eyes, not understanding why none of the wisdom can penetrate. I choke back crushing waves of panic, my whole body goes numb, and the *fear*, the mind like a runaway train, all lost, marriage gone, parents humiliated, love evaporated (was it ever there?), where do I move to, the city is too expensive on a teacher assistant's salary, what about the thesis? Abandon all? Run away to India? Ridiculous. Please don't let me end up at my parents' house. *Failure.*

Vanderoe pokes his head into my office. "Join me for a bag lunch in my office," he insists. "Noonish?"

I nod meekly.

At twelve-fifteen, I slog over to his office. He looks even larger than usual, his torso made bulky by a thick, cabled wool sweater. Something his wife Anna might have knit for him. His pencil holder holds only a toothbrush and a tube of paste. I feel like I'm looking at a still life. Vanderoe pushes a manuscript across his desk at me. It is his recently completed book.

"Read it," he commands. "Let me know what you think."

I lift the manuscript from the table. It must be at least four-hundred pages. The title is *The Passionate Greek*. I skim the preface.

"So you've written a scientifically based book about passion in ancient Greece?"

"Yes, it's the kind of approach I've been urging you to take. How close are you to finishing?" Vanderoe asks me, insistently.

"Close. I've got two more chapters and the conclusion."

Vanderoe looks at me dubiously. "It's February, as I'm sure you are aware," Vanderoe says. "Has the committee gotten your draft? Have I? What's going on? You haven't shown me anything in a while." He chews on his sandwich. "I'm not extending your deadline," he says.

"I'm not asking for an extension."

He sips from his drink, one of those juice boxes you see all the kids with in the playground that screams "No sugar added. 100 percent fruit juice."

"Self-doubt, questioning the purpose of life, irritable bowel, phantom illnesses. Get over it. If you don't want to do it, if you don't have what it takes, quit. I know the symptoms. Every doctoral candidate falls victim to them."

"I have every intention of finishing on time," I say, getting angered now that he's assumed that I won't.

"You have a good thesis. If you are ambitious, you could turn it into a book. Don't get hung up on that existential stuff.

Get the chapters to me next week. I need to see pages."

"Okay."

"Anjali," he says. "I've got kid No. 2 on the way." He lays his hand on his manuscript. "This isn't about inspiration in the moment. It's about getting up at four a.m. every morning, working until seven, getting the baby bottle ready for Davis, jogging two miles, spending all day watching my back in these hallowed halls, then getting back to work on it until midnight."

The more Vanderoe pontificates on his modus operandi, the more I want to cup my hands over my ears. He and Zoo. Their demands, opinions, arrogance. Somehow, I don't know how, I have to escape them. Run. To him. My blue skin lover. To embrace him and be lost in the compassion of his gaze.

I refocus on Vanderoe. Collect the remains of my lunch and toss it in his trashcan. Play the game, Duck told me.

I smile. "Congratulations! Another baby. You are very admirable. I'm not sure anyone can live up to your standards. But you've inspired me. Thank you."

I see his chest puff up like a bird that has had its feathers preened. I pick up the book. "I can't wait to dig into this. I'm honored that you are letting me have a peek at it."

The book is ridiculously heavy.

"I think you will enjoy it," Vanderoe says proudly. "It's got some holes here and there regrettably, that no doubt the critics will pick up on, but it's my best work to date."

"Wonderful."

I walk out of his office and down the hall to my own. I flip through the pages of Vanderoe's manuscript. It is studded with graphs and charts and even odd formulas that look mathematical. He has quantified the Greeks. I wonder if I wandered into the men's bathroom I would find him there brushing his teeth with rigor and precision, hitting the deep grooves of the molars two or three times. I wish for him a visit from my lover. So that all that is really hidden in the chinks between his teeth, and more important, the crevasses in his soul, can really be flushed clean, revealed. It is clearer to me than ever that the secrets of the ancient world cannot be quantified, or maybe even analyzed. At best we can surrender in awe. Like I did. With *him*.

I return to the dark apartment where a gloom has settled over everything. I don't turn the lights on. The message light is blinking. Let it. In the bedroom, I light incense at the altar. I say his name ten times. *Om Nama Shivaya*. I crawl into the womb of my bed; it's the safest place I can be, comforted in the darkness of evening and the heavy weight of the comforter. Minutes or hours pass. I can't tell.

And that's where he finds me.

I hear footsteps and think, oh god, Zoo changed his mind and didn't get on the plane this morning. What now? I wonder. An emerald ring? Does he think that will buy back my affection? He can't be that deceived.

I smell the first hint of jasmine, and I hear the wispy strum of sitar. I listen more carefully. Another cascade of beautiful notes. I peek from the cover. Golden sparkle fills the air.

And it's him. At the foot of my bed.

He fills the room with his incredible blinding radiance. What I see is a man who is lit as if from behind so that I cannot make out his features, only the perfection of his form. He is tall and straight with a sculpted torso and thin waist, long arms, and wonderfully bony knees.

He jumps on the bed and the covers fly off like birds taking flight. Ash rains off him. I don't know if I am ecstatic or terrified. I feel too exposed, too naked. I grab the covers and pull them back over me. I wait breathlessly. Grasp for bearings.

He pulls back the covers. In a flash, he has transformed into an ordinary man. Gone the cobra, the exotic garlands, the heavy golden ornaments. He is a simple man with a blue T-shirt as I first met him at Jangles' side. His eyes pull magnetically. He extends his hand and waits for me to take it. I do.

37

We sit together on the floor, cross-legged, two yogis at work. His legs weave together effortlessly. His long arms rest on his knees. His hair is wound in a topknot. Up close, his face is a little unnerving. It's the lack of facial hair or any blemish. His eyelashes are impossibly long and sweep upwards, his eyebrows arch like bridge supports. My own hands resting in prayer in front of my heart.

> *Not one or two or three or four,*
> *But through eighty-four thousand wombs*
> *I've been born*
> > *Again and again!*
>
> *Each time, unwanted*
> *Prey to wanton desires*
> *and painful bondage*
>
> *Forget those births!*
>
> *Show me your mercy*

O lord white as jasmine
Just this once

Eighty-four-thousand births! Sitting here with him I feel timeless. The great burden of *today, right now* has lifted. Which birth am I at, I wonder. Am I new born, or old soul? I ask him.

What do you think? He asks me back with his kind and curious gaze.

Somewhere in between, I speculate. It's the safe answer. At 42,250? I laugh. How unnerving. What is the meaning of all these lives, these endless cycles of birth and rebirth?

Each birth, he tells me, brings the soul closer to the One. When you are one with the One, then you are free.

When he says *free*, I feel a surge shoot through my heart. As if I didn't even know how immediate, how pressing the need was. I stare into my lover's forceful gaze. It is so bright, it hurts. He has brought me right back to *now*.

I am not Akka. I am not even close.

He repositions himself behind me and wraps around me. His legs fold around my own. His arms surround my shoulders and my chest. He holds me like that, and all I feel is a gentle flush of warmth, like a bath at just the right temperature. His breath drapes me in a cloud of luscious scent. We sit like that for a long time. He doesn't stir, and I don't either, yet every pore in my body is open, every sense in bloom, even my bones seem to be singing inside, my teeth happy in their homes, my eyes floating, my face soft and pliant. I have never felt more alive.

38

I pull him down,
and dig into the rich dark coils.
Loosen the plaits,
as I navigate his lips.
Trident, cobra, tiger skin, flashes of gold, rivers in his hair.
As the clock ticks, the second hand moves one notch.
He doesn't waste a moment.
His thighs straddle my waist.
He breathes fire down my throat.
He transforms from man to god.
I don't even really see it happen, the way a hologram shifts from
being to non-being.
I'm impatient to rip open the mystery of this lover.
Each muscle is taut and he is ready for my fire.
How will you make love to me today? I whisper.
I want to know.
He laughs!
His four hands cavort with my breasts.
He wants to play

Like man and woman,

vertical,

horizontal,

and like God,

in this dimension

and other ones.

Among stars, and grassy fields, and wisps of clouds, like a changing kaleidoscope of time and place.

I am flirting with danger; I know that.

I cannot pretend to be whimsical and cute.

It is a question now of tearing my heart out.

I tell him I want him to lash my hands together,

and untie my breath.

Let it pulse and heave like a tigress in my chest,

and let my tongue beg for more of whatever he will give me.

All night,

all day,

clueless,

careless,

bare-skinned,

brown and blue.

He tells me I am the very dance he has been waiting to perform.

Once we lock in embrace, he tells me, we will continue our play for three million years and the gods will all become angry because there is work they want him to do.

He has put aside all work to be my lover.

Aha! I exclaim. I can't resist him. I surrender my lips, and his taste is sweet and spicy.

He says, *Anjali, your name means offering.*

So this is how two souls have been brought together.

His intention is my dance; his prayer is my command.

His blue skin will be my downfall.

39

He stands before me. But he's not alone. He has a crowd with him. Standing next to him is Parvati, silken skin, liquid eyes, curvaceous hips. And next to her their sons; Skanda and Ganesh, unmistakable with his elephant trunk. And Ganga, his second wife, glistening with dewdrops of water. And on the other side of him, Sati, his first wife, in a simple red sari. I gasp. The air is filled with sparkle and golden light.

Parvati takes my hand and holds it out to Ganesh, who takes a pen and inkwell from the folds of his cloth and proceeds to write in deep black ink across the top of my hand. My lover reads the words as Ganesh scripts them in dark ink. *Take knowledge from the ancients, seek your true course, liberate yourself from bondage.*

He writes *Om* in one beautiful flowing move.

I look into Parvati's eyes, so feminine. Her hair long and lustrous like his. Her countenance oozing with powerful energy. And Ganesh, so fat, so generous, so loving. Skanda's boredom, dragged along like a teenager. He brought them all. To help.

The sparkle and light lead me to my desk. I look at my hand, and it's smooth and blank. In my head I repeat the words Ganesh has written. *Take knowledge from the ancients, seek your true course, liberate yourself from bondage.*

Akka Mahadevi's name stares out at me. I have buried her alive in a tomb of words.

Write with your heart, and not with your head, my lover tells me. He sits across from me like a well-paid tutor. He has left his finery behind; he is simple and unadorned. The others dissolve as they have come, leaving just him.

I stare into his face, which shows neither compassion nor judgment. "Help me," I plead.

I am here, he says. His blue stain pulses on his throat. I take his hand and place it over mine as I guide my pen to the blank page in front of me.

Akka had two weddings, we write, hand in hand. *One to the King when she was thirteen, whom she fled from. The other to Shiva, her Lord White as Jasmine. Her choice this time.*
The great Allama Prabhu, the most saintly of the Shiva worshippers, performed the wedding ceremony. Married her like a nun to Jesus Christ. All the Shiva worshippers were witness.
There was no question now of her devotion,
Or her purpose
Or the path of her life.

I stop mid-sentence. I want to know why he married her.

He gets a look in his eyes. *A marriage brings two souls together,* he says. *There is no Shiva without Shakti.* She is Parvati and Ganga and Sati and Akka. *She is all my wives. She is you.*

I startle. Me?

Where was I before he entered my life? Those unnamed tremors and longings. The emptiness that left me feeling like ashes in the fireplace. The sense there had to be more. My lover's eyes offer me, in their whitish glaze, peace and silence. I kiss him and empty the pain I feel into his lips. Touching his ears, I feel the warmth carried in sunlight. I have felt myself expand in his presence, felt myself go from a frayed fabric remnant to a piece of cloth joined into a larger quilt, stitched on all four sides by threads that run the whole universe deep. I have doubted myself. Denied him. Yet he didn't go away.

I stare down at my thesis. I can inhabit Akka's story now. Chapter by chapter, I can illuminate an unusual society of poets and saints and their followers who sought to keep the union between men, women, and their gods out of the oppressive hands of ritualistic orthodoxy, the rule makers and the power hungry. Who created a short-lived utopia where the unsullied bond between nature, man, and God would be honored and celebrated. And in that midst, Akka, long-haired naked saint, lived out the very word of their beliefs with her own highly personal response. Her quest for the freedom of her spirit, as deep and eternal as human life itself, played itself out in the most extreme of circumstances.

I write non-stop. I write as if in a hot fever. I flip back and forth through different chapters of the thesis making connections where before I could see none. I am at one with the scholarly knowledge I must dispense, following the rules of academia like an obedient pragmatist, footnoting and appendixing as needed. In a nod to Vanderoe I even acknowledge that one day scientists may discover a "religious" gene within the human mind. But until that time, I argue, the strongest evidence for our need to connect to that which cannot be named exists in the wealth of writings and literature throughout history. I feel *his* power in me, but it is my own will that pushes me forward.

40

Zoo calls. His bedtime, my teatime. The sound of the phone ringing draws me up as if from underwater. I've taken only short naps between writing. When I looked up, he was long gone. He left me to my work. Lover, whose love seared words on a page. I don't know when he left. The sparkle and glitter died out long ago. The sun went down, and it came up again. Maybe twice. I brushed my teeth and thought of Vanderoe's bright blue toothbrush sitting in his cup. His book lay like a corpse on the table and served the useful purpose of reminding me what I am up against.

Zoo's voice is cheerful and bright, as if being across the ocean has obliterated the undercurrents and weeks of tension.

"Happy anniversary, darling. Did you get the flowers?"

"No," I say. "What flowers?"

"The flowers I sent. Damn, I can't believe they didn't deliver them." He sounds angry and upset.

I walk with the phone to the door and open it. I remember the buzzer sounding, but in the fog of my mind, I had ignored it.

"The flowers *are* here," I say to Zoo. "I must have not heard when they delivered them." I set the phone down and carry them into the apartment. It's a huge bouquet of exotic and ornamental flowers. I place the vase they came in on the coffee table, and they stare back at me like one of those gifts that says "if this doesn't work, I don't know what will."

"I hope they're beautiful," Zoo says when I pick up the phone again.

"They are," I respond simply.

There is a long silence. We listen to each other breathe.

"Are you alright?" Zoo asks.

"I'm working hard," I tell him. "I feel like I can make it."

"That is wonderful," he says enthusiastically.

"I don't care if he fails me. I'm writing it the way I want to."

"He won't dare fail you," Zoo says.

There is another long silence. I want to hang up the phone. I can't carry on pretending like this.

"How long are we going to keep on fighting?" Zoo says.

"I don't know."

"I know you're angry about the apartment. But I know you will be happy once we're there."

"It's not just that." But I can't complete the sentence. I'm too exhausted.

"I know it's a crazy life. But it won't be like this forever. I promise." Zoo yawns. "This conference sucks, by the way."

"I'm sorry." I feel anxious to get off the phone. "Isn't it your bedtime?"

Zoo yawns. "Yeah, my eyes are shutting as we speak."

We say our good nights, and I set the handset in its cradle, and it clicks with a dull thud. The apartment is fast getting dark in the shortened day. I don't like this hour. It scares me. I stare at the thick volume of pages in front of me. I don't know how I will face Zoo's return. What can I say, after all? Am I ready to call it quits? Thinking about it sets off another wave of panic. I want *him* back. I want to be lost in the luxury of his eyes.

41

Mary calls and wants to get together for dinner and drinks and dancing. Ed is with Zoo at the conference in Brussels. She knows I'm alone, and I hear a tinge of desperation in her voice. I suggest just dinner, a neighborhood Italian restaurant.

She shows up twenty minutes late. I wonder what could be the matter. She unwraps a long red scarf and sheds her matching red winter coat. She orders a glass of wine, and now I order one, too.

"Do you miss Zoo," she asks, "when he is away?"

Why is she asking me this? Does she know something?

"Usually," I say. I sip my wine and look at Mary. "He missed our anniversary." Safer to keep it harmless girl talk. I don't mention the new apartment. Or the lover.

"I don't miss Ed." Mary's voice is full of venom.

"What's wrong?" I ask, although I think I already know.

"I'm going to ask Ed for a divorce," she states.

I suck in my breath.

The waitress is back to take our order. Mary fingers her

ring. The diamond sparkles in the light that shines down from the ceiling fixture. It makes me look at my own ring, two small diamonds inset on either side of a larger one, an antique inheritance passed from Zoo's grandmother.

Mary's news tastes like lead. "Does Ed know how unhappy you are?"

"I'm done, Anjali."

"What about marriage counseling?" I ask.

Mary winces. "Why do we need someone to help us figure out we don't belong together. Problem is the fucking Catholic Church. We're going to have go through all that annulment crap."

"Is that difficult?"

"Hell yes."

The waitress sets our food in front of us. Mary pushes the noodles around on her plate and takes the tiniest bite. Her phone sounds off and by the way she turns her head away from me and the way her voice changes on the phone to a low kind of sexy, playful voice, I begin to suspect what has happened.

"Is there someone else, Mary?" I ask her as soon as she finishes the call. I don't know why this wasn't the first thought that occurred to me, but now it seems so obvious.

"Don't tell Zoo, okay?"

"Who is it?" I ask.

"He's the contractor who is doing our apartment. He's fun. We've gone dancing a couple times. You know what I say. Fuck this marriage shit! Fuck everybody and everything. I'm sick of it all."

I can picture Ed's devastation. The way his eyes will fade and recede. The baby's room will have to be wiped off the plan.

"You're not going to get down on me, are you?" Mary asks, pinning me. Her lips are taut, glazed with her trademark orange lipstick. I look down at my plate. How can I condemn her? I'm not any more innocent than she is. The only difference is I'm not looking to switch Zoo for some other Zoo.

"You have to tell Ed," I say.

"I know. I will. It's just that I'm a coward."

Talking with Mary is like looking in a mirror. I see myself reflected back in every word she says.

42

Z oo comes home today.
Girls, my bridegroom comes home today
Let's wear our garlands
Let's make ourselves pretty

I have cleaned the kitchen, stocked the fridge, changed the sheets, folded the towels with hotel precision, plumped the pillows, neatened the magazines, dusted the books, and even vacuumed under the sofa. I haven't been able to sit still. Because when I tell him the truth, it is going to hurt.

He's coming now!
My lord white as jasmine
Welcome him!

I wait at the windows. Look down on the avenue. Buckets of rain douse the city. Five degrees colder and it would be snow. I wait for a yellow cab to pull to the sidewalk. And one does. There he is. Zoo. He pays his money. Disappears into the vestibule.

I open the door. He brushes my lips with his. Wheels his suitcase to the kitchen counter. Travel weary.

"How was the conference?"

"Just swell."

There's a sharp edge to this voice that wasn't apparent on the phone the other day. He sifts through the mail. Can he see the unhappiness lurking in my eyes? How do I begin the conversation I know I have to have.

"And you? How are you?" he asks finally.

"Me? I'm fine."

"Lovely. Got wine?"

I reach into the sparkling, hygienic fridge and pull out a bottle. Zoo takes over, removing the cork, pouring the wine. He looks around the apartment.

"Something is different here," he says.

"I cleaned," I say.

"Did you have people over?"

"No."

But a look of suspicion inhabits his face.

"Are you hungry?"

"Don't talk about food," he snarls.

"Is something the matter?"

"You don't want to know—"

"I do."

He takes a big gulp of wine. And then another. "Two of my clients are being investigated for fraud."

"Jesus."

"The fucked-up thing is that they were handed to me by Silver. So stupid of me," he says, fists clenched. "I should have seen it coming."

"But it isn't your fault—"

"OF COURSE IT'S MY FUCKING FAULT!" Zoo's body goes rigid. His hands fly in the air. He smashes his foot into the closet door. The sound reverberates like a gunshot. "I've been set up to take the fall. I knew something was fishy, and I didn't follow my gut."

I remember the dinner. Silver's measured smile. He probably was reading Zoo's eagerness. Playing him. Wondering if he'd take the bait. He took the hook without a second thought.

"What a bastard," I say.

Zoo looks at me with rabid eyes. "There is no way you can understand this. You don't have this kind of pressure sitting on your head. You don't pay for all this. You can sit on your ass for five years writing a fucking dissertation."

I spin on my heels and head into the bedroom. I crash on the bed and choke on everything that is bottled up inside.

43

We meet in the morning in the kitchen. Zoo slams the silverware drawer shut. I've lain awake all night, my mind in turmoil. He has given me the perfect opportunity.

"Zoo, I'm sorry about your work," I say, hoping that by starting soft I can make things easier. "But this isn't working for me. Maybe we have to think about a divorce."

The words come out rehearsed and stiff. Zoo looks at me for a minute.

"Fuck you," he says.

The phone rings. Perfect timing.

He answers it, and I can tell instantly that it is his mother. Something about a visit. More perfect timing. When Zoo hangs up he tells me they are coming to town.

I don't respond.

"Did you hear me?"

"Yes."

"Then why didn't you say anything?"

"What do you want me to say? Yipee."

"In any case we're going to have to have dinner with them. Or is that asking too much?" His sarcasm is blood curdling.

I boil inside.

Zoo folds the paper up and grabs his briefcase. He's out the door and neither one of us bothers to say goodbye.

When he leaves, I pray at my little altar.

Om Nama Shivaya

I hear his voice, or is it my own? *Pass the test. Pass the test.* "What is it? What is the test?" I am anxious to take it, to succeed at it.

He asks how much I am prepared to sacrifice?

"What do I need to sacrifice?"

Everything.

What I pray for is knowledge and for answers. I pray for all the pieces of the puzzle to come together.

44

oo phones and says he is stuck at work, can I go ahead to the restaurant where we are meeting his parents and he should be there by dinnertime. I respond to his request with an extended dark silence. I consider not showing up at all. But I dread all the questions that will follow, the misplaced anger. It will just be another thing Zoo will hold against me instead of the real thing, the thing I cannot explain without explaining *him* which is impossible.

Roger and Mimi are waiting at the restaurant when I show up. They look around and practically through me to see where I'm hiding their son, who as a child they had little interest in, or at least that is what he claims.

"Won't Niles be joining us?" Roger asks.

"He will be late. He had a work emergency."

They can't hide their disappointment.

"I should think everyone is scrambling a bit," Roger says. "What with the economic situation."

I've forgotten how tall they are. They preside over me like king and queen. Roger seems older and frail. I feel the distance I always feel in his presence. Mimi's face is plump and gorgeously pink.

We settle down for drinks and review the six months since we last saw each other. Dreadful winter in London, gray and cold, wonderful holidays in Spain, Guggenheim in Bilbao is fabulous and the Spanish absolutely know how to live. They inquire after my parents, and I tell them all is well in Chicago. I don't tell them about the new job my father was forced to take. Despite Zoo's confident proclamation that my father would not lose his job with the merger, he did. His new job has entailed a substantial cut in pay.

Mimi tells me her book on native plants will be forthcoming in May. There have already been some write-ups in horticultural journals, and the native plant movement is finally taking hold.

"We're working very hard on a national strategy, you know," Mimi says, ticking off the key areas of prevention, early detection, surveillance and monitoring. "I mean, you wouldn't believe the battle we've had with *Fallopia japonica*, Japanese knotweed. We may have lost that battle, I'm not sure."

Roger puts a hand on her hand. "Darling, maybe this isn't so interesting to Anjali."

"Invasive non-native species of flora and fauna are considered the second biggest threat after habitat loss and destruction to biodiversity worldwide. I'm sure that is of interest to Anjali," Mimi says defensively.

"That sounds so horrible," I say, feeling grateful to Roger at the same time as thinking that I am so tired of all this, of feigning interest, of being the good daughter-in-law. I tell them I finished my thesis, and now it is in the hands of the committee. They raise their glasses in a toast.

Zoo finally shows up, his tie knot loosened, his shirt no longer fresh. He looks irritated and jumpy. He kisses Mummy and nominally hugs Daddy. I study my menu silently.

"How's business?" Roger asks Zoo as he settles into his seat and spreads the napkin over his lap. The waiter hurries over and takes his drink order, a vodka tonic.

"Business is business," Zoo says.

"You look weary, dear," Mimi says to her son.

"That I am," Zoo says.

When the waiter comes to take our order I have thought far too long about what I want to eat here, studying the menu as if it is a scholarly work. I've changed my mind twenty times, and now nothing seems appealing, so I order a salad and a baked potato. Zoo and his father order steaks as big as their plates and Mimi orders native Long Island clams and a side of seasonal vegetables.

"Anything new on the horizon?" Roger asks.

"Actually yes," Zoo says. "I've bought a beautiful apartment, but it looks as if only one of us will be moving."

My whole body goes cold and frozen.

Mimi and Roger look puzzled.

"Where is this apartment?" Roger finally asks, when Zoo offers no explanation.

Zoo describes the apartment, the view, and explains the financing and how it is an excellent investment. He doesn't mention the crisis at work, how Silver set up him to take a fall. Or that his wife has suggested they get a divorce.

Roger immediately jumps on the bandwagon. Thinks it sounds like a marvelous opportunity, although it's just across town and not to London, where they would really prefer to see us relocate.

"Why don't you like it, dear?" Mimi asks me.

Where to begin? How can I explain that I'm dying on the inside. That, like a big chunk of iceberg, I've broken off and floated away. That I don't think it is all my fault or Zoo's, but the cracks were there all along, and we didn't see them.

"He just did it. He didn't ask me."

"Niles, why didn't you ask Anjali first?" Mimi says.

"Maybe because I wanted to surprise her with a really big Christmas present and show her that I love her and care for her and want to make babies with her and all that good stuff." Zoo glares at me.

"Now, now. I'm sure you two will work it out."

Roger saws the last bit of his sirloin. Mimi puts her hand on mine. "I don't mean that children are a solution to a marital problem, but maybe you two should think of it. I mean, they can help."

"Are you sure you could love your hybrid, non-native grandchildren?" I ask.

"Anjali! That is uncalled for!"

Mimi looks to Roger who shifts uncomfortably in his seat. Roger signals for the waiter. "Refills on water, please. And the check. Coffee? Dessert?"

45

I lean my head back on the taxi-cab seat. I want my blue skin lover. He is my ticket out of this.

"If you think I'm going to let you off the hook for being rude to my mother, I'm not. I'm sorry if you can't be happy with the nice fucking life I'm providing you with. I am having fun, most days. The question is what is the matter with you?"

The cab smells of dirty socks. I long for bed and sleep.

My head hurts when I wake up. A wave of nausea drives me to the bathroom. I didn't think I had drunk that much. I hope I'm not coming down with a flu. Zoo is in full motion in the kitchen. The quick flip through the *Wall Street Journal*, the *New York Times*, the ritual of the coffeemaker, and a bowl of cereal. He acknowledges me with the barest of nods.

I look at the kitchen, and I would like to take my arm and sweep it clean of everything: the blender, the Cuisinart, the electric knife sharpener, the toaster, the utensil caddy, the knife caddy, the paper towel holder, the cookbook holder, the rice cooker, the electric frying pan, the electric wok, the waffle maker, the bread pan, the mini television, the dust buster, the CD player, the clock radio, the key cubby, the twine holder, the egg timer, the free to-do pad from Groening Bros. Plumbers, the cute monkey magnets, the incredible chopping gizmo my mother sent me.

And then I feel it. I look at the calendar. A missed period. Then I know. The sickening certainty that I am pregnant.

46

A quick pharmacy test confirms my fears. My head swirls. It is as if a tornado has just swept me up, foundation and all, and landed me in a whole new place. A place I don't want to be. I know I should call Zoo and tell him, but I can't pick up the phone.

I close my eyes and whisper *his* name. I try to sink deeply into that place, deep in my breath, where the noise of my mind can dissolve into silence. The place where I can most often find him, where the light is gentle and washed in heavenly pinks and blues.

He comes as a beggar, hunched over, clutching a walking stick with one hand and holding a begging bowl in the other, and wearing a necklace of skulls. He would be frightening, this old man in ragged cloths, except his face is peaceful.

He holds his begging bowl out to me.

I take the bowl wordlessly.

I go to the kitchen and prepare simple white rice. He sits at the kitchen counter, slipping his fingers over the worn beads of his mala. Because he is so grandfatherly, I feel I can ask him the question that is burning in me.

Should I leave Zoo? Not have the baby?

He sucks me into those grandfatherly eyes. I am embarrassed to bring my earthly concerns to him.

You should do your duty, he tells me.

My heart tightens. I raise my eyebrows. To whom? To Zoo? To my parents? To you? Or to myself?

Isn't it all the same? He says gently. Why do you distinguish one from the other?

I can't see how it can be the same. I feel as if my mind is being twisted into a pretzel. My marriage vows spelled out my duties, *for better or worse*, but my heart is bailing. Zoo provides for us, he certainly does his duty, and I have everything I could possibly want, an academic career, a more than comfortable apartment, time for family and friends, and now a baby. *A child.* How do you run from that? Yet restlessness is digesting me from inside to out. I crave to fly on the power of my own wings.

The rice cooks quickly, and I scoop it out of the pot into a bowl. The old man suggests a little ghee would be nice. I reach into my cupboard and pull out the small bottle of clarified butter. I dollop a spoonful onto the rice and hand it over. I watch him eat. His bony fingers work the rice into a perfect ball. He eats with grace and doesn't stop until his bowl is empty.

I ask him if he would like a little more, but he shakes his head. Unlike me, his hunger is easily satisfied. There is a lesson in that. He strokes his beard. He asks me if I understand the nature of devotion?

In this moment I don't understand much of anything.

That's what I tell him.

Do what I do, he says. He sits up, tall, with his head balanced perfectly on his shoulders and back, better than any yoga teacher I've ever seen. I follow. He brings the palms of his hands together in front of his chest. Prayer position. His long, tapered fingers, wrinkled and withered, glimmer in the dim light of the room. I do the same. *Close your eyes.* I do. And then I feel him reach over, and his hands enclose mine like an envelope encasing a letter. I fight the feeling of being held prisoner. Why do I feel this way? *Duty, devotion*—the very things I have wanted to leave behind. We sit like that for a long time. I can feel each fall and rise of his breath. I resist the urge to break free. I open my eyes and gaze on his face. It is absolutely serene. His eyes are closed. *Close your eyes*, he scolds. I smile. That is not devotion, I tell him. That is obedience.

Then show me devotion, he says.

I feel a rush of anger. Gods, husbands—they are all the same.

As if he can read my mind, he changes into his divine form and hovers an inch off the ground. His arms are crossed, and he has a wild look in his eyes. *Didn't you invite me?* He seems to be asking.

I suggest to him that the nature of my devotion has not been right. What is all this lovemaking, this descent into the carnal? What spiritual enlightenment is there in that?

Do you think it matters if I enter you through the orifice of your lower parts or the gaping orifice of your mind? The Gods have cavorted with humans from time immemorial. You are our play-

ground, you exist for us to fiddle with, and we exist out of the bounty of your imaginations.

So you are just playing with me? I have the violent urge to smash everything in sight. I want to rip him apart. Everything about my life would have been perfect in this moment if he had never showed up. I would have finished my thesis, been blissfully happy with child, settled into a new home, and on and on. But now the taste of the life I thought I wanted has soured like milk gone bad. I want to be free of him. Of everything.

I have only to think it, and he's gone.

And when he leaves what is left is the silence of me, alone. I sit at the edge of the chair in the kitchen and lay my head on the cold stone counter. I don't move for a very long time. Traffic rattle and the chopping of a helicopter overhead. The clunking of the elevator in its shaft. The metallic screech of brakes. A siren wailing its way down the street. Was it just a lover's spat? No, more than that. The wretched person in me cannot unglue herself from the misery she has wrought.

47

I drag myself to the theater where Mimi and Roger have gotten great seats for Broadway. We kiss and greet as if nothing has happened. Zoo excuses himself to take a call on his cell phone. They complain about the traffic gridlock in New York City, but praise their taxi driver, an African man, who promised to get them to the theater on time, and drove like a maniac, swearing in Swahili the whole way. Mimi says she kept her eyes glued shut. Roger tells me he was wonderful. I tune out their easy chatter.

When Zoo returns, he tells them I'm sorry for what I said last night. He looks at me pointedly.

"Yes," I say. "Sorry."

"Don't be silly," Mimi says. "I do go on a bit too much about that native stuff. I never meant it to be taken the way you took it. Heaven forbid."

"Yes," Roger says. "Mimi is the most tolerant of people."

The lights blink three times in the lobby, and we head into the theater. Zoo confronts me as soon as we take our seats.

"Where were you when I called at lunchtime? His voice

is a hissed whisper.

"At lunch," I say.

"You never go out to lunch."

"Not true."

"Tell me the last time you went out to lunch!" Zoo's face is red and puffed with anger.

"I can't remember." I have no energy for these arguments.

"Who did you have lunch with?"

"Vanderoe," I lie, although I did see Vanderoe when I finally made it into the department and returned his book to him and told him it was brilliant and inspiring. I read the first two chapters and two in the middle and the final two. He told me he was going to get to my dissertation in short order.

"What does he want?"

"My opinion of his book."

The house goes black. The curtains pull back.

"He wants to get in your pants."

"Jesus Zoo. That's disgusting."

The actor strides out. Applause.

"I heard what Mary's up to. The contractor. Disgusting."

Now I understand the jealousy, the accusations. It has nothing to do with me.

Roger leans over and hushes his son. The actor's voice booms out. The play is a comedy about the end of the world. Rejoice. All the world's a stage.

48

Except it isn't. I wake up the next morning with another wave of nausea. I rush into the bathroom and lean over the toilet.

Zoo calls out from the bedroom. "Are you okay?"

I almost never throw up.

"What's going on?" he asks as I exit the bathroom. He's still in bed.

"I'm pregnant," I tell him, standing in my stocking feet in the middle of the bedroom feeling chilly. Saying it out loud for the first time makes it more real than when it was just a fact in my head.

I can literally see the news sink into him, like a stone thrown into a pool, and when it hits bottom there is a silent thunk.

He sits straight up. And then a huge grin erupts on his face.

"Really? How do you know?"

"I did the test."

"When?"

"Yesterday."

He jumps up and down like a kid. He whoops it up. He twirls me around.

I feel limp and helpless in his arms. I can't share his joy.

"Why didn't you tell me?"

"I just did."

"But right away."

I sit down on the bed. We review how it could have happened. I am always so careful.

"We've got to get you a doctor. Better someone on the East Side. Closer to where we are going to be living. Probably want to have it at Mount Sinai.

Zoo picks up the phone to share the news.

"Put down the phone!" I scream.

He sets the phone down and looks at me with a kind of puzzled confusion.

"You can't tell anyone. It's bad luck until the first trimester is over." It's true, I've heard my mother and her friends talk about this. And I've known other women who miscarry and then there's all the awkwardness of explaining to everyone that there will be no baby after all. But Zoo keeps looking at me. As if he knows.

"You do want to have this baby, don't you?" he asks finally. His eyes penetrate me with a determined question mark.

49

I can barely breathe in the trap that is closing in on me from all sides. The sick twist of fate.

My body is dust,
My soul empty
      What can I hold onto, Lord?
      How can I know you,
Lord
Free me from my delusions,
lord white as jasmine

Dear lord, dear Akka, free me from mine, too, while you're at it.

But I know what happened to her. Death. The thought of it makes me weak with fear. She became restless in the city of rebellious saints. She was close to her mystical vision: union with the divine. *Moksha.* The ultimate liberation. The moment when the mind no longer needed the body because it had reached the state of pure knowledge of the self.

My body
Is nothing
My life
Is beyond
My heart
Has no will
I am yours
I am one
With the Absolute.

Her final pilgrimage was to a famed Shiva temple hidden deep in a mountain range. She traveled there to seek ultimate enlightenment. *Nirvana.* She walked for miles, accompanied by a group of devoted pilgrims. They reached the mountains of the Eastern Ghats, dense thickets of forest along steep ridges and plateaus. At last they came to the temple called Mallikarjuna, where the story was told that a young girl, not unlike Akka Mahadevi, was visited by Shiva in a dream and he told her that he was present in a stone by the river. She built a temple in the spot and offered jasmine flowers there every day. It was said that the devotees' truest desires were granted at the temple.

Akka and the pilgrims worshipped there for days, but then it was time for the pilgrims to return home. She told them she would stay on. They couldn't convince her otherwise. At the bottom of one of the gorges lay the Krishna River, shimmering like a silvery braid. They watched as she descended deep into a treacherous cavern. The stories say that tangled vines ripped into her skin. A tiger watched. Snakes dropped from trees. She entered a cave and settled into fervent prayer.

She followed the six-stage path of devotion and surrender: *bhakti, mahesha, prasāda, prānalinga, sharana, and aikya:* devotion, selfless service, earnestly seeking Shiva's grace, experience of all as Shiva, egoless refuge in Shiva, and oneness with Shiva. She reached the moment of true union with Shiva, the ultimate goal of the spiritual seeker. She begged Shiva to give her release from this life. All she wanted was his kindness.

And to be one with him.

50

I t hits me with a jolt. The urgent need to see Jangles. Consult her. I try to think when I last saw her, maybe two weeks ago. Maybe three. Maybe more. I'm sure the winter weather has kept her away.

I walk into the grocery store next to where she sets up shop, but the old man who is usually there isn't. I ask the cashier, a young kid, probably the owner's son, if he knows anything about the old woman who sells stuff on the corner, but he shrugs indifferently. I rush home. Somewhere is the card that Jangles handed me eons ago. I remember saving it. I check first where I stash the bills, but I can't find it there. I rifle through all the drawers in the kitchen, through the stacks of magazines on the coffee table, in our bedroom among the items on the bureau. Finally, I find it buried on the nightstand next to my bed. Thelma Boatwright, Church of the Eternal Good Word, it reads. I try the phone number, but there is no answer. The church is way uptown.

I head out the door. The sky is darkening quickly. I catch the A train. It's still rush hour and there will be plenty of people about. When I exit the train, I look around. It's rough here. The storefronts all have bars, and graffiti decorates every brick wall. I step around broken glass on the sidewalk and hold my breath as I pass an overflowing trash bin. There's a corner grocer, and I walk in the dark entry. There's a feeling of life having seeped out; half the bulbs are blinking. I find a man half-hidden behind cartons of cigarettes and ask for directions. He mumbles something, and I'm afraid to ask him to repeat. I think he said it's about ten blocks away.

I head out and up the street. Most of the shops along the street are closed. And then there aren't any more shops, just apartment buildings, mostly three and four stories. Some are boarded up completely, and some are burnt-out shells. I think about turning back, but I can't now. The need to see her has become a scream in my head. I feel as if she will know what I need to do.

Few of the buildings have legible addresses. I come to a brick building like all the others. I peer up at it. It doesn't look like a church. The door is painted black, but most of the paint has peeled, and the wood has turned gray. The windows have heavy bars over them, and no lights burning inside. I walk up the steps and buzz the doorbell, but there is no answer. I ring again and wait. I knock. My heart is pounding. Finally I hear a voice respond through the door.

"What you want?" The voice is of a young child.

"I'm looking for Thelma Boatwright," I reply.

There's a long silence.

"Does she live here?"

I'm met with more silence.

An old man wearing a little bowler hat shuffles up to the building and walks through the black gate that descends the stairwell to the basement apartment. He knocks on the door, it opens, and I hear the sound of singing filter out. I rush down before the door closes. An elderly man with a neatly trimmed mustache is guarding the door. He is stooped and bent.

"Can I help you?" he asks, drawling. He seems to have a hard time even holding his head up.

"I'm looking for Thelma Boatwright."

"You know Missus Boatwright?" His voice is gravely.

I nod. "Yes, I'm a friend of hers."

He raises his head with effort and looks me over. He looks back into the room. The singing is steady and melodic.

"You wait here," he says and closes the door.

It seems an eternity before the door opens again. It's Jangles. She looks shocked to see me.

"What'cha doin' here, girl?" she says, her voice loud and warm.

"I was worried about you. You haven't been around."

Jangles smiles. "You came all this way to check up on me? Lord. I'll be damned."

"Are you okay?" I ask, although I can see with my eyes that she is fine.

"Are you?" she asks me back and leads me through a long dark hallway.

The singing gets louder as we walk. She leads me into a dim room with low ceilings. There is a hand-scripted sign on the wall that says Church of the Eternal Good Word. Folding chairs are arranged loosely in a circle, people hold black cloth-bound books in their laps. There is an upright piano and a straw-hatted skinny woman sitting on a bench in a dress with the Eiffel Tower printed all over it as if its flying through space. All the people are well past sixty. They are of African-American descent, like Jangles, and like the piano player, attired in formal dress and all manner of hats. Jangles looks like an odd sheep in this crowd with her clumsy layers and her odd turban topping and bangles up her arms. She shows me to a chair and takes a seat next to me.

The voices are real and throaty, high and low, and beautifully harmonious.

Sweet Jesus this, and Lord save me that. Jangles' voice next to me is powerful. It moves me with its soulful grace. Her eyes are shut, her lids swollen, and her face covered with a delicate sheen of sweat. The group switches from one song to the next under the direction of the tireless piano player. On the wall next to me is a large paint-by-number portrait of Jesus. The bottom corner has been left unfinished, showing blank areas and coded numbers.

I stare into Jesus' suffering, beatific face. The spikes, the red blood dripping down the palms, the long straggles of hair, the naked torso. His body bread, his blood wine, God's sacrificial lamb. Seeing him, I think of my lover. They are both beautiful men, replete with feminine grace, but the eyes and nose and expression are entirely different. I miss my lover's smirk and the way a sense of playfulness lights up just behind his eyes. And his love. That I have banished.

Jangles rises next to me. She moves to the front of the room. All eyes are on her. She begins to talk. I watch as they listen to Jangles. Their faces are etched with the lives they have lived, some with drooping jaws, others from deep lines across their foreheads, others with canes propped against their legs. The words seem to bring a sense of peace to them. My lover never offered me comfort, only the challenge to abandon comfort.

There is a greater sin than hiding secrets from God—
Jangles voice bellows out with power.
And do you know what that is?
Tell us, her congregation responds. *Tell us, Thelma.*
Hiding secrets from yourself is a greater sin!
That's right!
Her words pierce through me.
Dealing drugs and telling folks you are a businessman.
That's right!
Cheating on your wife and telling her you're out playing cards.
That's right!
Beating your child and saying he needed it.
That's right!
You can lie to everyone else, but the lies you tell yourself will strike you down! Only one person can catch you in that lie, and that is yourself! Revelation 21:8

Jangles turns my way. I'm almost ashamed to look at her.
The truthful lip shall be established forever, but a lying tongue is but for a moment.

Her eyes don't let go of me. What does she know and

how does she know these things? Have I even admitted these things to myself? Jangles has ripped the blanket off me, and I am left shivering in the cold. I look away from Jangles, because I can't bear the intensity of her gaze anymore and the instant I do, I know what she is saying to me. I know I heard what I needed to hear.

I have been lying, and now I must tell the truth.

51

As the subway rattles home, I sit in an almost-empty car. I can still hear the singing of Jangles' congregation in my ears. All those faces, wrinkled and shaped by lifetimes of experiences. Knowing Jangles' story, I can imagine that theirs are just as convoluted, and that they have crossed just as many rivers. They give me courage and strength.

When I walk in the door of the apartment, it must be almost ten.

"Jesus, where have you been?" Zoo asks. He's sitting at the dining-room table with his computer in front of him.

"I went to check on Jangles. She hasn't been around."

"Ah, the saint. Saint Anjali, helping her poor, down-trodden friends."

"Zoo—please."

I sink into the sofa. I lay my head back and close my eyes.

"Say something, goddamn it. Don't fucking tell me you don't want this."

"I don't want this," I say, barely above a whisper. Even

though my voice is quiet, I know that there is no way I can continue this life. I cannot, no matter how wide the path of hurt will be.

"What do you want?" Zoo says, barely containing a scream.

The sound of his voice reverberates like an echo in a canyon. Want, want, want, want, want. I sit immobile on the sofa like an old animal in its cage. Akka gave up everything.

I answer with the truth. "I want to be with my lover."

Zoo's face registers what looks like a shock wave. First he squints his eyes to look more forcefully at me, then his mouth contracts into a sickened grimace. The expression rips through me.

"What did you say?"

I walk into the bedroom. Zoo follows me.

"Don't walk away from me!" he yells.

At my altar, I take the Shiva lingam and hold it in my hand. I extend the lingam towards Zoo. "This is my lover."

Zoo snorts. "What the hell is that supposed to mean?"

I know I am inadequate to explain anything to Zoo. We are past explaining.

Zoo takes the lingam from my hand. He looks it over as if it were nothing more than a ninety-nine-cent purchase. He tosses it on the bed.

I start to undress, facing Zoo full on. He backs away from me. The last piece of clothing, my underwear, comes off. He continues to stare at me. I see the confusion in his eyes.

"Jesus, what game are you playing?"

I take some ash from the incense holder and paint three stripes across my forehead.

I sit on the floor, cross-legged. I close my eyes. I call my lover's name.

"*Om nama shivaya.*"

Zoo shakes me by the shoulders. His hands are rough and strong, but all he gets from me is my lover's name.

I chant quietly. Will my lover hear me? He heard me before, but that seems a million years ago.

"*Anjali.*"

Zoo says my name. It sounds as if his voice is deep underwater, floating past me like a slow-swimming shark.

"I'm ready," I whisper.

"*Anjali.*"

Is that my lover's voice I hear? I say his name at least two hundred more times. Sooner or later he will hear me. It's impossible to believe he has forsaken me. It was I who abandoned him, and now I must get him back.

52

Morning comes. Somewhere in the night I lay my head down on the floor. Zoo must have covered me with a blanket. My head is thick and hurts, my body stiff and old. Hair has matted against the wetness on my face.

Zoo has a small suitcase on the bed, and he's packing it. He sticks in a swimsuit. I watch and count as he takes five pairs of clean socks from his drawer. Five shirts go in. And then pants, already folded on hangers. Two sweaters. A suit goes in a separate garment bag. It must be a business meeting. He stuffs a book he's reading, a biography of T Boone Pickens given to him by my father.

I don't feel sad that he is leaving. Or happy. Or angry.

"I'm not the wife you want," I say.

"And apparently I'm not the husband you want."

He goes in the bathroom and returns with a bag of toiletries and presses it into the suitcase. He yanks the zipper around the bag leaving a great smiling metal lip.

He lifts the suitcase off the bed and looks at me. "Get

your head screwed on straight, and then we'll talk."

"And get some clothes on," he says and walks out the door.

I pick myself up off the floor. I'm hit with nausea as soon as I rise. I run to the bathroom and disgorge into the toilet. The mirror shows me the same silent face it has always shown me. I am flooded with disbelief for what I did, telling Zoo, revealing myself. My tongue swims in sludge. I look down at my brown skin, my wrapping, my naked body. Run my hands over my belly. Deny what I know is true. My body now has another agenda. I offered it to Zoo so willingly, let him unearth its secret desires and it responded with union, with child. So why does he want me to cover it up now? Because I have driven him to hate. I saw the look in his eyes, as if he was looking at a convicted criminal, a child murderer. I earned it. I stopped playing nice, but it was more than that. I stopped playing.

I rinse out my mouth, but the taste doesn't go away. Telling the truth is one thing, living it another.

53

I wander outside. I can't face myself. I want to find him. Get him back. He is my last resort. I placed all my bets on him, and I want to collect. Manhattan without my lover is an altogether different city. I remember when he walked alongside me and played with me, blowing temperate gusts my way. The heaviness of the buildings presses in on me; the trash is unbearable; it was winter yesterday and now spring is crawling over the dead branches. Nature doesn't care if wives leave husbands. Her indifference is soothing. The sun relaxes into the shadows. Clouds drift. The wind whips up.

What will I do without husband, home, work, family? My lover told me to sacrifice everything. I have. I am poised to face the empty plate, the blank page, the existence without bonds. Where is he, the one who promised to reward me with his love.

I search for him in playgrounds.

In alleyways.

And hotel lobbies.

And in the zoo.

Maybe he is hiding behind the tiger's eyes.
My blue skin lover—
For the attention he gave me,
For the fire he breathed in me,
For the minutes he was able to stretch into an eternity
of bliss.

I'm turned upside down
The breeze is on fire
The moonlight burns me like a hot sun

Like the tax collector,
My work is never ending

Please, friend, let Him know

Bring Him here, dear girls
My lord white as jasmine

He is angry
That we are two

Gone, the lustrous blue skin,
The thick coils of hair,
The golden touch.
I wait on a park bench and say his name a hundred times,
but he doesn't come.
I watch dogs catch Frisbees and tourists pay to have
cartoon drawings of themselves.

I watch the skate boarders crash and burn, and listen to
children beg for more ice cream.

Parrots with your constant chatter

Have you seen Him or haven't you?

He wants nothing more to do with me.

I am not worthy.

I have hardly demonstrated my devotion.

Cuckoos, singing your silly songs

Have you seen Him or haven't you?

I have enjoyed him as if he was the dessert.

As if I could have both

My cake

And eat it

Too.

Bees that dart and play

Have you seen Him or haven't you?

I pick petals from a chrysanthemum that has survived
the winter.

Meant to be.

Not meant to be.

Love him.

Love him not.

Loves me.

Loves me not.

Tell me, o tell me

Where he is

My lord white as jasmine

54

L over, I'm calling your name. I have more incense lit than a Buddhist temple. I sit before my altar with only one thought in my mind. *Devotion.*
Om Nama Shivaya.
Om Nama Shivaya.

Behind the dark lids of my eyes, I see Akka in the cool wetness of the plantain grove, sheltered in the lush giant plants with their feathered leaves, listening to the call of the twittering finches singing in the mountain breezes. She has come to her final destination. She has sent all others away and insists on being alone. In this most holy of places she receives the enlightenment she seeks so desperately. She decides that she can leave life itself. It is said that she sat and prayed until she dissolved into a shower of light. She attained the blessed state of nirvana, bliss, and moksha, liberation: she became one with Shiva, her lord, white as jasmine.

Om Nama Shivaya.

Maybe she was eaten by a tiger. Maybe she slipped on a rock and fell into a mountain crevasse. Or maybe she just starved herself to death. Praying. Being one with him.

I chant to him. My blue skin lover. I have never felt so alone in my life. He doesn't come. All the calling of his name does not bring him to me. I sent him away and now I am being punished. I have not been a worthy disciple. I have been too wishy-washy, one moment wanting him, the next afraid of his terrifying hold.

Om Nama Shivaya, I call. Ten times in succession. Then twenty, then thirty. I am left empty-handed. Where can he be?

55

The next day, the city again. I will do whatever I have to do to get him back. I press my face to the glass of store windows hoping to glimpse him. Eyes stare back at me. Are they trying to hide him from me? I sit under a tree and wait. A dog approaches me. It is collarless and ownerless and aimless like me, sniffing by the trashcan, then at a bare patch of earth, then by the tree trunk. Maybe my lover has taken a dog's form. I reach my hand forward, but the dog snaps at me. It barks with a short staccato yip, forelegs braced, neck arched forward, ears taut. I rush away. How far I go, I'm not sure.

I pass Nails, Nails, Nails. I decide to go in and say hello to Le Ly, the girl who worked on my nails. I want to help her somehow. Maybe if I help her, he will come. But her station is empty, and when I ask the other two women where she is they tell me she's doesn't work there anymore. Not enough work, they tell me. "Bad, bad economy." I somehow wrangle an address from them. I stop at the bank and withdraw money.

When I emerge from the subway station I recognize nothing. The streets are heavy in shadow, the sidewalks broken and unrepaired. Le Ly's building is decaying tenement brick. The halls smell like reused fried oil. The stench of urine is inescapable.

I walk up to her apartment, five floors up, breathing hard. I knock on her door twice before she opens it. She steps back, shocked to see me. I ask her if I can come in; I want to talk to her. The television is on loud, and I see her child sunk deep in the sofa, like an egg in a nest.

"Tran!" Le Ly calls. "Tran!"

He makes no move to her. She walks over to him and scoops him out of the sofa. He protests, his eyes peering over her shoulder not to miss whatever action is happening in the cartoon. Le Ly brings him over to me. "My friend," she says to him and smiles.

"Tran three-year old," Le Ly says. "Show friend three finger," she says to her son.

I could be the abominable snowman, the way he pinches his face. One good look, and he begins to howl. I am deeply embarrassed. Le Ly sets him back on the sofa where his cry turns to a whimper, and his eyes hollow once again to the television. She gestures for me to follow her. She opens a door to a room quietly and slowly, and then wider. An old man is in bed. A small bedside lamp glows yellow-orange. He is sitting up and staring at the footboard.

"This my father," she says.

I whisper a hello. I nod my head. He nods to me. He is shrunken, and his skin is the color of yellow apples. He holds up an empty glass next to him. Le Ly takes it. I follow her back to the kitchen where she fills the glass with water.

The kitchen is the size of our coat closet. A wok sits on the stove. Le Ly invites me to sit at the table. She tells me she will be back in a minute. I feel calmer, grateful to be with a family. My gaze shifts all around the apartment. Le Ly and her husband must sleep on the sofa with the boy. Her father is in the only other room. There are posters of beaches with palm trees and men on bicycle rickshaws. I'm pretty sure I've seen these same posters in Vietnamese restaurants. The table has a plastic tablecloth, a deep maroon color. A vase of plastic flowers decorates a corner table, but the flowers have gone dull. The shades are pulled down over the windows in what seems to be a permanent arrangement. A movement on the stove catches my eye, and I see a cockroach dart in and out from the burners.

Le Ly re-emerges from the bedroom. She is helping the old man shuffle to the kitchen. He has on a bathrobe and slippers. She seats him at the table.

"Once upon a time my father scholar. Very smart man in Vietnam."

I can easily recognize the intelligence in his eyes. I am familiar with the way book learning inhabits people's faces and bodies, the knitted brow, the hunch in the shoulders, the chin perpetually craned upwards. And there is the gleam that you don't see in businesspeople or even doctors or construction workers.

Le Ly puts water in the kettle and sets it to boil.

"What did your father study?" I ask.

"He study history of Buddhist Vietnam. Write book.

Famous in Vietnam."

The old man nods. He points vigorously to the bedroom and mumbles something in Vietnamese. His voice is hoarse.

Le Ly goes back into the bedroom.

"Do you speak English?" I ask.

"He shakes his head back and forth. "No speak," he says. His hands are trembling. He smells of flesh rotting from the inside out.

The teakettle rattles on the stove. I can smell the gas.

Le Ly puts a book bound up in an old cotton cloth next to her father. His hands tremble as he fumbles with the knot to untie the cloth. I restrain myself from reaching over. Finally, he succeeds and reveals the book. It is a thick tome, bound in a plain red cover. He hands it to me. I turn the pages carefully. They are thin, slightly better quality than newsprint, and the binding is weak. The book is fragile, a precious thing. His life work. To be honored and held sacred.

He takes the book back from me and reads the inscription in Vietnamese. His voice is different now, as he reads these words written long ago. It has strength and tone. I look to Le Ly for the translation.

Le Ly hands me a cup of tea. It is fragrant, the delicate scent of jasmine.

"Beautiful life is known only by knowing opposite." She struggles to find the right words. "Something like that."

I nod.

The door to the apartment turns. It is Le Ly's husband. My presence shocks him, and he stands in the doorway holding two shopping bags unable to speak for a moment.

Le Ly helps him, apparently, because he nods to me, and I nod back. He goes to the sofa, and Tran comes to life, happy to see his father. They wrestle on the floor, and Tran makes little yelps and screams of delight.

It is time for me to leave. I feel big and burdensome, just being here.

"Le Ly. This is a thousand dollars. I want you to have it." I place the envelope on the table in front of me. I have not had a moment of doubt since I decided that this was the very thing I must do. I push the envelope towards her. She rests her hand on it. Her husband walks over to the table and asks her what it is. She speaks rapidly in Vietnamese. I see his face turn a reddish color. He unleashes a slew of angry words at Le Ly. She cringes. She has tears streaming down her cheeks. The old man just sits in the chair, looking as if he is preparing to speak, but he says nothing.

Her husband pushes the envelope back to me. "We don't want your money."

My face stings. This is not how I envisioned this happening. I wanted to feel good about helping someone. "No, no," I say. "You don't understand. It's for Le Ly. She is my friend."

Tran pulls on his father's pant leg. He wants his father to play more. His father looks at Le Ly. She looks at me. She hands me the money. "We don't need your help," she says. "Maybe you give to some poor people."

I get up to leave. I will not take the money back. I back away from the table and into the door.

"Just keep it," I say desperately. "Do whatever you want with it." I try the door handle, but it is locked. I urgently turn the locks, but the door doesn't open. Le Ly's husband comes to the door and turns one of the locks. I'm shaking now. I just want to escape the apartment, the building, and get back onto the street where I can breathe. The old man is coughing, and Le Ly holds a handkerchief under his mouth, looking at me all the while with a sorry and confused look.

Her husband opens the door, and I spill into the dark hallway. I find my way to the stairs and rush down the five flights. Outside, I head to the subway, walking fast. A gang of five young teenage boys claims the sidewalk as they walk towards me. Their black clothes blend with the dark night. I'm not afraid. I don't care what happens. Let these boys take what they want. A knife deep inside, would it be so bad? I'm not scared to end all this. I miss my lover terribly. He, the creator and the destroyer, worked his powers on me. I am guilty of betrayal. I have been stupid and delusional. He would have been here to protect me if I had not pushed him out the door.

As they get closer, I see their faces. Ripe babies, that's all. They part in two groups at the last minute so I can pass through them. I smell their pungent male scent. I hear their laughter behind me. A light rain starts to fall. I welcome it. Steam rises up from the sidewalks.

I wander all day. Dark comes. The park is quiet. Maybe he will be there. No. Only trees that don't move, and joggers who don't stop. I can't stop my mind. I want him; I need him; I am nothing without him. When I think of my life with Zoo,

I am certain I was dying. Something in me was decaying. My spirit. Even if it wasn't his fault, I am angry.

I know. By the river. Warm breezes funnel up from the water. The pink and green oily water invites me as it moves relentlessly forward. I need to quiet the turmoil inside. The riverbank is empty. If I tear my clothes off, be naked like she was, I will catch his attention. Why not? What does it matter now? I have been a coward and a liar. I take my socks off. My bare feet absorb the cold of the concrete embankment with a shock. Then my shirt. My bra. My bare skin shivers in the open air. My hair gets whipped by the breeze. It's not nearly long enough to even cover my breasts. Who cares? My pants. Waves rise and dip and crash about like over-energetic children at a playground. I think maybe he will rise up out of the water. I look deep into it, sure now I will find him. I am Akka and my great-grandmother and all those women before me who knew without a doubt that they could call on him when they too must have felt like living was dying. Should I jump in? Is that what he wants?

A man in a policeman's uniform approaches me. It is blue. I smile. Has my lover taken this form? Has he come finally? I feel joy. The man takes me by the elbow and asks me where I live. He takes me to his car. I think he is taking me to him.

56

I pray all day at my altar and still he doesn't come. I sit naked, and I say his name at least five thousand times. I weep for him to come back to me. My tongue is so dry and thick and heavy I can hardly move it. They say you can only get what you want if you want it bad enough. Maybe he is just another failure of my life. I put on my blue salwaar kameez. I don't want the policeman who is not *him* to bring me home again.

I find my way to Jangles at her corner as the sun is setting. She is back after her winter hiatus. Jangles looks me up and down. She clicks her tongue, but she doesn't ask me any questions. I love her. Maybe she will lead me to him. She collects up her business in two large plastic shopping bags. She takes her chair to the corner grocer where he will stash it for her this night. She folds up her cardboard throne and hands it to me.

"Carry this for me," she demands.

I am happy to obey her. I take the cardboard from her, and grime covers my hands and the sleeves of my shirt. I follow her down 98th and then through an alley and then back to the street, always keeping a few steps behind. Her big body lumbers and sways side to side like an elephant, and her turban sits high and mighty on her head. I shift the cardboard from arm to arm; it's not easy to carry because of its awkward size, and it bangs against my leg, but it's an easy burden compared to the war going on in my head.

We head uptown. A group of men at the corner are laughing and enjoying whatever it is they're drinking and smoking; I hear catcalls and don't look their way; I'm on a forced march, gratefully, and I don't look right or left. A teenage boy with super-baggy pants that barely clutch his hips gets between me and my view of Jangles, and for a while I watch the crack of his ass. My lover would find it a funny joke if I thought that's where he was hiding.

Twilight is fast disappearing. Jangles waits for me before she turns up another alley. I might see him around each corner, see him in the piles of broken bottles or maybe he will pop out of the orange trash container stamped with the name Bowman Sanitation. I hear the subway come above ground somewhere in the distance.

"You're leading me to him, aren't you?" I ask her.

"I'm just taking you home, honey," she says.

We arrive in her neighborhood, and the scenery becomes familiar to me, the broken buildings, the treeless streets. She steps through the black gate, and we descend into the stairwell of the building. She bangs on the door, and it opens at the hand of an elderly gentleman.

"Mrs. Boatwright," he says.

"Mr. Michael," she replies.

The man looks me over, blocking the door.

"Let her in," Jangles says, so he steps aside. I follow Jangles through the long hallway. I glimpse into the large room where we sat last time. The chairs are set up for the evening meeting, and people are just arriving, milling about, saying their hellos. Jangles prods me into the kitchen. She nods as she passes people. We pause at the kitchen sink, and Jangles hands me a cup, which I refill three times with water from the tap. She opens the refrigerator and pulls out a brown bag.

"Will you be joining us this evening?" the skinny lady who plays the piano asks Jangles.

I hide behind Jangles.

"Maybe later, maybe later," Jangles replies.

The piano lady looks at me. "This your friend?" she asks.

"That's right," Jangles says.

"She come on hard times?"

"Don't everybody, now and then?"

"Amen."

We go out the back door and climb the back stairwell to the top floor. We enter a small apartment that is dark and almost as frigid and cold as the air outside. There are no windows and barely any furniture. "Here we are," Jangles says. She sets her bags down in a corner, and I prop the cardboard against the legs of an old bureau. A cot is set up against the wall. An old piece of green rug edges out the cracked linoleum floor. Jangles pulls some blankets out from one of the boxes and hands them to me.

"Fold these up, make a bed for yourself," she says.

So I do. I fold them lengthwise and lay them down in a

neat pile near the cot.

"I'm starving," she says.

She pulls out a package of hot dogs from the small re-frigerator. She puts a small pot of water to boil on a hotplate that sits on a folding table. She asks me if I want to eat, and I tell her no.

"Suit yourself," she says.

Jangles picks her teeth with a toothpick. She hums a little. The sound is soothing.

"You left your husband, didn't you?"

I nod. I lie back on the thin bedding and stare into the dingy ceiling. I feel a different kind of ache. It spreads through my chest and throat. It is the ache of having walked out of my life, and now that I actually confront this thought, my whole body shakes; my throat is so tight I am afraid I won't get enough oxygen.

"What happened to that god you was trucking with?" Jangles asks.

I cringe to hear it put that way. "I lost him, too."

"You can't lose god."

"I did."

If I can just see my lover, if I can feel the heat of his intoxicating presence, I know I will be all right.

Jangles sings, her voice low and sweet and cracked.

You got to walk that lonesome valley
You got to go there by your self
Ain't nobody here can go there for you

"Don't stop singing," I tell her. Her voice resonates

against the thin walls of the apartment. I find solace in it. I want her to go on and on. She clears her throat and continues.

You will see the coffins bustin'
You will see poor sinners creepin'
Then you'll hear the hell hounds barkin'
With the rumblin' of the thunder,
Then you'll see the moon a-bleedin'
See the stars a-fallin'
See the elements a meltin'
And time will be no longer

You got to walk that lonesome valley...
You got to go there by your self.

"That's a beautiful song."

"You never heard that before? Old gospel song. My Mama sang that one song over and over. I heard it even when I was in her womb. Heard it as I was coming out."

I look at her trying to imagine my own baby hearing songs in the womb.

"You don't believe me?"

"Why wouldn't I?"

"Most people just don't. Don't believe you can see and hear in your momma's womb."

Inhaling in slow, measured breaths, I feel an urgent pushing within me. I feel it in the ache of my muscles, the heaviness of my heart, my lungs that want to burst through my skin, like a hot-air balloon readied for flight.

"I'm pregnant."

"Oh lord," Jangles says. She rises, and I startle to feel her seat herself next to me. She lifts my head and places it into her lap. With her two palms she covers my swollen eyes. I am flooded with her gentleness, her sweetness, her great tenderness for me. How did I ever find her? The tears come easily, and she allows them.

She sings her song again, and the low swoon of her voice permeates every pore of my body.

You got to walk that lonesome valley
You got to walk it by your self

I release myself to her mothering. Under the palms of her hands, every muscle eases. My face warms under the softness of her skin. I breathe slower. She is the womb I can crawl into. Her touch is a miracle. I listen to her song. Her heart beat. I travel with her voice as if I'm on a raft going down an easy river. My mind, like an egg in a bird's nest, feels only the smother of warm, soft feathers. I feel the fall into sleep.

57

An explosion rocks the morning and wakes me up forcefully. I don't know where I am until Jangles gets up in a panic. Seeing her, it all comes back to me. We hear another explosion. She goes to the door. I shake loose of my bedding and follow her. She climbs the fire escape to the roof. It is daybreak. The sun cuts the surface of the eastern ridge of brownstones. We rush to the edge of the roof, stepping over abandoned junk, and see a blaze exploding from within an apartment building across the street. Smaller explosions sound off at random. As if in slow motion, people begin to gush from the building into the street.

A great billow of black smoke amasses above. The shifting breeze carries the smoke in our direction. My eyes sting. My nostrils are inflamed. My throat burns with fumes. Jangles covers her mouth with her hand. I pull the bottom of my shirt up to my nose.

"I'm going down there," she says, her voice muffled.

I look down on the chaos, the different groups of people, pajama-clad children, bare-chested men, women dragging bags of stuff out, and feel leaden. I stand paralyzed. I don't know if Jangles expects me to follow or not; she just heads for the stairs and disappears through the rooftop door. What can I do? What help? What should I do? I reached out instinctively for Jangles when she had her heart attack, but I don't feel that same instinct now. I want to run away from all the chaos. I want to be free of it.

And then I see him in the smoke; I smell him; he is right in front of me; he reeks of burning buildings; his ash is everywhere; he dances furiously; his two legs stamp a hard-driving rhythm; his four arms fly like a great flock of birds, and his torso spins like a top gone mad to the beating of his drum; his dance makes the clouds race through the sky. It makes the buildings shake; it makes the ground rumble. I stagger backwards.

I am here. His voice booms in my ear. He is a lion, sated from the hunt, enjoying the flicking of his own tail.

"I've been searching for you."

He laughs, and his laughter detonates everywhere.

I am here. I have not gone anywhere, but you could not see me. His voice, like symphonic music, wells up, gathers all the discordant currents of the air and harmonizes them.

"I want to be with you," I tell him. "Take me away from all of this, like you took *her*."

It's difficult to look in his eyes; they are sharp and bright. He comes to rest. He sits in front of me, perched on the edge of the roof, the fire burning behind him.

His blue pulsates. His hair emanates shiny dew.

"What do I have to do to have *you*?"

Which part of me is it you want? Do you want my arms?
He detaches his arms and hands them to me.

I step back, horrified.

Do you want my lingam? He rips his penis off from between his loins.

I scream.

Do you want my heart? He reaches inside his chest cavity, as if it is a treasure box, and yanks out the full, beating heart.

"No! No! You are laughing at me. You who told me to
sacrifice everything."

I feel the mockery of everything I have done. Everything
I am. I step to the edge of the roof. I look down, the ground a
long way off. I want to jump. It wouldn't be so hard. One step
and I'm over the edge.

Do you want to see death? I can show it to you.

I turn to look at him again. His cobra arches her neck
forward, and her hood flares out; she strikes me with her mouth
on my neck so quickly I cannot even jerk back. I feel the poison
rush into me; the sky goes black, and I feel the rush of a hot air-
less wind; my feet are no longer touching earth; I am not moving,
but it is as if everything around me is in movement.

I am alone in this vast cosmic darkness. No lover, nothing. I look out into the universe of black, and there is no form
to rest my eyes on, no smell to sniff at, nothing to reach out and
touch. I reach out into the darkness and cannot even see my own
hand. Only my heartbeat thuds with complete clarity. Then, a
single corpse appears in front of me, the bones bleached, the
skull rigid with a gaping open mouth and scooped out sockets

for eyes. The corpse is stark white against pure cosmic blackness, like a black-and-white solarized photo. And then I recognize my own teeth, the way the bottom center teeth overlap. I am looking at myself. I lean over the skeletal remains of myself and touch the hard skull; I run my finger in the nose cavity; I touch the hard bony fingers that once were mine; I lift the arm, and the hand droops like a puppet without strings; I stroke the bones of the feet, and I know that wrapped around this skeleton is everything I once was, alive and breathing. But me, the essence of me, has dissolved away.

Nothing moves. The molecules of the air seem to float like butterflies adrift. If a clock was ticking, it has stopped. Endlessness is mine. I am with my own skeleton for an eternity. The brazen puppet does not offer any conversation. It just is. I close my eyes and inhabit a space I have never known before. I lie down next to the skeleton. This must be the place Akka came to. I know it in my being. Is this what I wanted? I seem to be crying somewhere deep inside myself. Crying like a little baby hoping someone will pick it up, hold it, comfort it.

Will you hide yourself within the lotus heart of my lord white as jasmine? I hear her voice first. Like clear music, the sweet lilt of a flute. I open my eyes and see her image emerge from the darkness. She carries a *diwa* in her palm, the flicker of candlelight soft and warm. I see her now so clearly. Lithe and small, with bony hips and skinny ankles. She walks as if weightless. Her hair hangs in long, vagrant wisps. She comes next to me, shining her *diwa* in my face. Her black eyes are a well of innocence.

Sister! It's as if we both say it at once.

Akka takes my hand and lifts me so that I am sitting up.

She circles her *diwa* around my face three times, maybe more, and all the while I stare into the compassion of her eyes. She presses her thumb into the middle of my forehead. I am receiving a blessing, her blessing.

Your life is written here, she says, pressing one hand into my heart. *And here,* she says. Pressing her hand into my belly.

I clasp her hand where it rests. Deep within we both feel the seed of new life.

What will you choose? she asks me.

What should I choose? I ask her.

You know, she says. *Because you have known him, my lord white as jasmine.*

58

The world I have known slowly comes back into being, like a mist rising; I see that the rooftop is underfoot, and the sun sits higher.

I have chosen.

The smoke of the fire is still rising in great black belches. I feel the sharp sting of it in my throat. My eyes burn. But my mind is clear. Alive. Fresh and healthy. I've gone through a terrible but good sickness.

I walk to the street below. I feel as if I am floating. I look down to see if my feet are touching the earth. Is he carrying me? No, I am walking on my own. I don't need him. I have chosen that, too.

I reach the street, and I see Jangles among the people. The fires have been extinguished and are smoldering. Crowds of people linger on. Jangles waves me over. When I reach her, she hands me a child to hold, a girl, who could not be more than five-years old, with big thick pigtails and dark, pudgy flesh. The girl grasps me around the neck so tightly I choke, and I have to loosen her grip with my one free hand, and I tell her it's okay, don't hold me so tight, I won't let you go. She rubs her eyes, irritated from the smoke, and I take her over to some steps out of the fray, and we sit together.

I ask her if she knows where her mother is, and she blubbers that her mother went in the ambulance with her brother. I wipe the snot from her nose on the tail of my shirt. I tell her that her mother will come back and that in the meantime I will stay with her and that seems good enough for her. She wedges deeper into my arms and soft sniffles continue in a steady stream.

Not too far in the future I will hold my own child like this. The baby that will be born will carry his mystery. My choice. Because that is what I want. I am ready. That is his gift. I was not ready for the plantain grove.

He is in me now. Friend, lover, troublemaker. He is a seed planted in my womb that will grow, use my bones for trellis, wash my face with tears, grow from my head in a bounty of hair, escape through my ears as warm wax, exit my mouth in a language I have worked hard to learn.

Zoo told me to screw my head on straight. There was a time when I felt I could see into his soul and he into mine. We lost that. I can't see how a child can bring us back to that place. It was no small thing that drove us apart.

The girl wriggles in my lap. Her hands grab me tighter. Her pajamas are rough and frayed.

"Don't be afraid," I tell her. "Your mother will come back. Are you hungry?" She nods. I am starving myself. I ask her where the nearest market is, and she points halfway down the block. As we get up, I stumble under her weight. She grabs my hips with her legs, letting me know she will not be walking.

"Have you ever heard the story of how a little boy got the head of the elephant and became a god?" I ask the little girl to distract her from the fire and me from her cumbersome weight.

She looks at me with curiosity. Her eyes are soft behind long curled eyelashes. Her breath warms my face. I tell her the story.

"One day Parvati, who is a beautiful goddess, wants to take a bath in a small hut in the forest where she lives. She has no one to protect her, so she makes herself a little son from the drops of the sweat on her body."

"How does she do that?" the little girl asks.

"With her magic powers, because she is a goddess." The little girl accepts the explanation. So I continue. "Then Parvati tells her son that he must guard the door and not allow anyone in, and she takes her bath. But then Shiva, who is Parvati's husband and a very powerful god, comes along, and he wants to go in and see his wife. But the little boy refuses. He says 'My mother told me that no one can go in.' Shiva becomes very angry. Still, the little boy doesn't let him in. So do you know what Shiva did?

The little girl shakes her head.

"He chopped off that little boy's head with his great big sword!"

The little girl scrunches up her face, horrified.

"Do you want me to continue?" She nods her head, eyes wide open.

"Then Shiva goes into the house and finds Parvati, and he tells her what he has done. Parvati gasps. 'Oh, but you've killed my son!' And Parvati cries and cries, and Shiva can't get her to stop. So Shiva rushes out, and because he is an all-powerful god, he breathes life back into the little boy. But the boy has no head! So Shiva sends his men into the forest and says 'quick, bring me back the head of the first animal you can find.'

"An elephant!" the little girl squeals.

"Yup. The first animal they see is an elephant, so they cut off his head and bring it to Shiva, and Shiva sticks that head with its long trunk onto the body of the little boy. And the little boy became known as Ganesh. And guess what? He became a god, too."

"I like elephants," the little girl says. "I saw them in the zoo."

"I like elephants, too," I say to the little girl, and to myself I murmur thanks to Shiva for chopping off my head and putting on a new one with which to see the world.

59

I hold little baby chubster in my lap and feed her mashed rice pudding, made with love by my mother. She eats hungrily, and I can't believe what joy this gives me, to watch her lips smack together, and her miniature hands clasp and unclasp the air. She has big, dark, beady eyes and unruly auburn hair, which curls in random spurts, and little rolls of baby fat that inspire one of her many nicknames. We sit on the patio outside in the bright daylight, and around us big sprays of red and orange bougainvillea fall off the arbor of our rented cottage.

My father is videotaping this momentous event, the *annaprasana*, the first taste of solid food. My mother is fretting over whether I am giving her too much when she spits out a mouthful or too little when her mouth opens up like a hatchling, and she bounces on my lap asking for more. I hand the spoon to my mother, so she can take her turn, and she coos and clucks as the baby takes the rich milky pudding into her mouth. I don't think I've ever seen my mother so happy.

My parents have rented an apartment nearby, and they are enjoying their extended visit to the California sun. The move, made just after the baby's birth, courtesy of my new job in Dr. Veeraswamy's Department of Religious Studies, has worked out well for all of us. It's a gift to have them nearby to take care of the baby when I'm at work, teaching, translating, and preparing my thesis for publication.

Later, I'll transfer the video of the baby to the computer and email it to Zoo in London where he too has a new job, new friends, and a new life. The emotional heat of our battles incited by the requirements of the legal settlement—how much, parenting schedules, where, when—the *why* now unimportant—has cooled, and we are now both focused on the logistics of giving chooki chubster a proper set of parents, the miles of land and ocean like a long scar between us that can only be healed by time and the curious bundle of life we've brought into the world.

At two months we had her *Namkaran*, the official naming ceremony. Dr. Veeraswamy and his wife came, along with a few others from the department and other mothers and babies I've befriended. My mother cooked a feast. Zoo flew in from London and Nita from Atlanta, who, holding the little *rani* queen, exclaimed, "I want one of these!" I held the baby in my lap, and everyone took turns blessing her, circling the little oil lamp around her face and dotting her forehead with red *kumkum* powder. My father recited the prayer to Ganesh, and Zoo tied the black thread around her waist to ward off evil spirits. At the appropriate moment, I brushed my lips to her ear and whispered her name to her. Jasmine.

The name fits her so nicely. I have planted jasmine all

along the picket fence, and already the vines are tantalizing us with prolific bloom. At night the fragrance is so delicate, so strong. One day I will tell Jasmine the story of how she got her name, and I'll recite her my favorite poem.

> *When I didn't know myself*
> *Where were you?*
>
> *Like the color in the gold,*
> *You were in me.*
>
> *I saw in you,*
> *Lord white as jasmine,*
> *The paradox of your being*
> *In me*
> *Without showing a limb.*

Every day when I look into Jasmine's eyes, I feel Akka, big sister, looking with me. I know the Ancients are here, Jangles, in spirit, is here, the lover is here, and together they will guide me. The household of the cosmos is here, and I entered its door, and I too am here, an ordinary woman marked with the ash of life.

ACKNOWLEDGMENTS

I must first thank my father, Kameshwar Wali, for telling me the story of the mystic poet Akka Mahadevi and for giving me the translations of her poetry by the wonderful poet and writer A.K. Ramanujan in his book *Speaking of Śiva*. I wish I had been older when Ramanujan was a frequent guest at our house in Chicago. I am indebted, too, to Roberto Calasso for his inspired retelling of Hindu lore and scriptures in the book *Ka* and to Wendy Doniger's brilliant and insightful work on the Hindu deity Shiva.

I wish to express my deepest thanks to Jim Krusoe, my guru, who illuminates the writing path with such brilliance and generosity and whose reading of this book was critically helpful and saved it from an unhealthy obesity. Most special thanks to Janice Shapiro for walking the writer's path with me every step of the way and for her friendship and love. With gratitude to Bob Richardson for providing for our family while I wrote this book and for his early enthusiasm for it, and to Alexandra Wiesenfeld for reading every draft and never once flagging in her conviction of its worthiness. Over the years, I have relied on the friendship and support of so many dear friends including Bob Dawson, Jill Neubauer, Parminder Vir and Sally & Bill Fletcher who have always seen the best in me. I was fortunate to have been born to the most loving, enlightened parents—Kameshwar and Kashi Wali—and to share my life with wonderful sisters—Alaka and Achala Wali. I have counted on my family every step of the way and there is no way to adequately thank them. Finally I thank my daughters: Kanchan, for the beautiful cover art, and Maya, for making me look good in my author photo, and because they are my sweet nirvana.